ORANGES A

Stories by gay men

Edited by
David Rees and Peter Robins

Third House (Publishers)

First published 1987 by Third House (Publishers)
35, Brighton Road, London NI6 8EQ, England

World copyright on the collection   ©   Third House (Publishers)
1987: on each individual work   ©   the author 1987.

Story editors David Rees and Peter Robins

ISBN   1–876188–00–4

Photoset by Rapidset & Design Ltd, London WC1

Distributed by Turnaround, 27, Horsell Road, London N5 IXL

WINTER LIGHT

David Rees

It was the life-long ambition of Mr Millwall (nickname Uncle Barry): a religious play performed in a church. When I found out what *Everyman* was I said it was crazy doing such a thing, an ancient play nobody would understand, in a draughty, freezing old building! And, worse, it wasn't to be in St Chad's, our nearest church, but St Giles, which meant hours getting there before rehearsals could start. St Giles was in the old village, a long dark walk down a country lane. I decided I wouldn't have anything to do with it, but luck was against me: Uncle Barry came to my house one Friday evening. I was out; 'Tony would love to be in it,' my mother said. She was raking the ashes in the front-room grate at the time. 'Of course he would. I'll tell him when he comes in. He's at Scouts.' So there was no getting away from it. I protested, of course, but my mother said I couldn't let him down. She had promised. She was very good at appealing to my better nature.

But there was one consolation: Tim Crane would be in *Everyman*. Just the thought of him sent strange fingers fluttering through my stomach. He was not in my class at school – he was a year younger – but we travelled in on the same bus. One morning on the bus, as I was revising for a geography test, he slipped into the seat beside me and said, 'Have you heard about *Everyman*? Mr Millwall said he was giving you a part. I've got a part.'

I was curious. 'Which one?'

'Beauty.' He giggled, blushed, then said, 'Rumour has it

. . . he wants you to be the Angel.' He lowered his voice. 'I hope you get to do Strength.'

Any thoughts I might have had about the possibly interesting reasons Tim could have for wanting me to be Strength went out of my head as I considered the prospect of being an angel. No! Never, not even if my mother went down on hands and knees! However, I tried not to show what I felt and kept my eyes on the page where it said how many tons of coffee Brazil exported in 1927.'

'I don't think he'd want me as an angel,' I said. 'Unless he's really hard up. No, Peter Davis is the boy for that.' Peter Davis was the red-faced cherub who had played Puck last year. People called him 'Grease' and he sang in the school choir, very sweetly and clearly, so that everybody could hear. 'Peter Davis,' I went on, 'is the only person I know who would enjoy being an angel in a crackpot play.'

'Yes, I expect you're right,' Tim said, meekly.

Rehearsals took place in the church at what was normally my tea-time. Although I got off the bus outside our house as usual, I had only a moment on these occasions to go indoors and leave my books, then I would have to hurry a good mile down the lane to the church. I longed to stay indoors, sprawling on the sofa in front of the fire with the television on, while my mother made the tea. Never again would I let her speak up for me. After all, I was fifteen and nearly the same height as my father. However, I did not have to go to very many rehearsals, for my part was only a small one – relief, relief, when I heard what it was – the messenger; but, unfortunately, Tim wasn't in my section of the play, so there wasn't any consolation in looking forward to him being there with me.

Once I had forgotten my irritation at having to leave the warmth of a good fire, I used to enjoy that winter walk. There was snow in November that year, and the land was hard with frost, grey with it, frozen and still. Trees on the horizon were as finely printed on the sky as if someone had just breathed on a window and the frost had formed them out of the breath. Behind them, the sun, a huge plate of orange glass, slid slowly down, and the shadow of the trees it threw onto the white fields' edges was like another

Jack Frost pattern of criss-crossing. My own breath was smoke in the air and my fingers and feet and ears throbbed with blood. I walked very quickly to keep warm, the hot damp of my body reminding me all the time that I was the last thing alive in this iron landscape; I was alone, trekking over an ice-covered polar sea, or crossing a glacier in a second Ice Age, but alive. . . Then the lane began to slope sharply downwards into the wood and the sun's plate disappeared behind the growing hill opposite. The silence was total now; the streets where I lived were out of earshot, buried – it could almost be a thousand miles away – the other side of the hill behind, and just as remote when I thought of it were the clack and squawk of all of us at school, seven hundred adolescents eating together and swarming about playgrounds and corridors and classrooms. The stillness made me think the trees were listening, though it's difficult to know how a tree can listen. In the quiet dusk their shapes were very like human gestures; heads bowed and branches raised in supplication. The frost ran its mark all along them to the ends of the twigs, made rigging on their trunks and whitened the arthritic joints of roots. It was then that I began to worry about wild animals that might be lurking in the shadows. . .

Once up the steep track and out of the wood there was the orange and scarlet left by the sun and the distant street lamps to reassure me. But entering the church was like returning to the gloom of the wood, particularly if I was the first to arrive, as I often was. The quiet here was vast. As soon as the echoes from the door banging shut had ceased, silence smothered me in a flood like the sea and I sometimes began to doubt my physical reality; I was just a walking head or mind or spirit in the presence of invisible shapes that could notice my slightest breathing. In the distance the sanctuary lamp glowed a dull red, but it was no comfort to me, an unbeliever; it was not the light that shineth in darkness, but only an old red lamp a bit like a Christmas lantern. Then one of the other people required for this rehearsal – Death (Clive Smith), God (Ian Bond), or Everyman himself (Don Roberts) – would open the church door, a sound far off like waves on a distant beach, and the

7

spell would be broken. Once again I was Tony Holt, flesh and blood.

Barry Millwall would arrive last. He was never known to be punctual for anything. He was always a bit flustered and took a long time to find the right place in the script (for my rehearsals, it was the beginning; I spoke the play's first twenty-one lines and then my turn was over for the evening) and while he sorted himself out, loose pieces of paper – his comments on the production, letters, pound notes – would fall about the floor like a snowstorm.

'Lights!' he would shout, and someone would turn on the lights in the crossing, for this was where the play was to be acted. This made the rest of the church even darker than before; from being a dimness in which it was possible to fumble from object to object the blackness was now impenetrable, a solid wall beyond the first five or six pews, and the church became higher, wider, and longer in my imagination.

'Right, Holt, off you go, laddie.'

Laddie! Ugh! But out I walked from the vestry, pretending I was some important medieval personage, richly-coloured robe sweeping the ground, whereas in reality I was shivering in my overcoat in an icy unheated church. In school we were doing some Shakespeare at this time, and once or twice I wondered whether to frighten Uncle Barry out of his wits by walking up to him and addressing him in ringing tones with the speech we were made to learn for homework:

> Good tidings, my Lord Hastings, for the which
> I do arrest thee, traitor, of high treason.

But I never quite dared; at the last minute I would swerve across the acting area and mount the steps of the pulpit as I had been instructed. Then I would start:

> I pray you all give audience,
> And hear this matter with reverence

and Uncle Barry would jump up from his seat in the front pew. 'No, no! More emphasis on *reverence*! Try it again!' And so on. At last, hours later it seemed, when my voice

8

was dry, there would be no comment after my last line and I could slink away down the pulpit stairs, while God, who was standing on the altar (the vicar said he didn't mind this, so long as Ian had clean feet), thundered out his tirade against the wickedness of mankind.

'Can I go now?' I whispered to Uncle Barry, who would nod, though he looked reluctant, as if he wanted to say, 'Stop and hear the rest. The play's superb; Ian Bond is marvellous. What could make you want to go?'

The plunge down into the wood was a very different matter now that night had fallen. 'You look as if you're being chased by twenty devils,' said my mother on one occasion, glancing up from her knitting; the fire crackled and the news was blaring from the TV: everything was telling me the real, comforting world still existed. She was not far wrong. In the quiet of the wood at night the tree branches were no longer the dejected limbs of the earlier walk; they were antlers with limitless, ferocious points; or, worse, the immense fingers of even more immense hands poised over me, ready to swoop, clutch and pierce right through. It was no good telling myself that it was all ridiculously childish, that if it was Friday I would be out after tea, in an hour's time, up behind the Scouts' hut, swopping crude jokes and having a drag with the others, thinking I was one helluva guy as I inhaled smoke deep down into my lungs. No – it was the nature of the darkness itself that upset me as I walked down into the wood. It was thicker, more absolute, than in the church; it almost gripped at my throat, and, as I made my way down the hill, trying to avoid the trailing twigs above me and the stones underfoot that could rick my ankle, grotesque images of faces – Greek masks that I had seen in a book at school – would form and hover in the air, there, and yet not quite there, like the Cheshire cat's vanishing grin in the Queen of Hearts' garden. So I would run, ignoring the possibilities of falling over the ruts or my face being lacerated by a bramble; I would still be panting when I arrived home, and I'd answer the inquiring look with, 'Didn't want to be late for tea' or 'Cross-country next term, got to start training.'

Time passed. It snowed a little and the frost held. Soon

the walk to the church was in darkness both ways and my running practice therefore had to be doubled; but as Uncle Barry continued to be late, I always had time to recover my breath before we began. At the dress rehearsal I wore my costume for the first time; it was a long greenish-yellow tunic that came down to the ground, and it quite lived up to my expectations. Its swash-swash noise on the floor was first-rate. The rehearsal was chaotic, for books were not allowed. Uncle Barry had tried, of course, to stop us using books days before, but the proceedings always ground to a halt when he did so in a shower of dropped cues and lost lines. On these occasions he was on the verge, nearer than I can ever recall, of losing his temper. Perhaps it would have been better if he had done so and let the church walls blench for a few minutes at his resounding roar of rage: his voice could carry, if he wanted, better than Ian Bond's. It sometimes did in class.

The day of the first performance, December the fourteenth, dawned auspiciously, for our first Christmas card arrived at breakfast-time. It was only Aunt Maud; she always posted early to remind those who would have forgotten to send her one back. But it seemed a good omen for the evening and I was grateful all day. I was not the first to arrive at the church this time; when I opened the vestry door, I saw medieval men and women talking and laughing, admiring each other's clothes – gowns and cloaks in purple, yellow, scarlet, olive green, beige – and adjusting hats; discussing Uncle Barry, how snobbish the Grammar School was compared with the Comprehensive, what an idiot the Headmaster was, how large the audience would be. Fellowship was in pink with dark blue birds sewn on his tunic in diagonals, like a St Andrew's cross. Confession, dressed as a Dominican friar, stood solitary in a corner, as if he were indeed meditating on the next world; he was a bundle of nerves and could not bring himself to speak to anybody. Five Wits straightened Good Deeds' hat, and Knowledge pulled up his tights, which were wrinkling just below the knee. Ash from a cigarette smeared the Angel's left wing, but Peter Davis – it *was* he – did not notice. Mr Wilson, our physics teacher and the stage manager, hurried through, waving a piece of paper. The cigarette vanished, but he noticed the smell, and frowned. Strength kept watch at the door and sent back messages, to say that the vicar had just come in, that Adam Charles, our electrician, was changing a bulb and that the first member of the audience, Mrs Gawn-Caine, had just arrived. (She had got the time of the performance wrong.) Soon an order came from Uncle Barry, who was fussing about with programmes in the church porch, and Strength shouted it over the noise: 'Will you be quiet! You can be heard in the organ loft!' The sound dropped for a few moments, then rose again to the level it was before.

As I changed into my costume I began to feel nervous. I don't know why people call it butterflies. With me it was more like having someone's hand round my heart, squeezing it; this was followed by a violent fit of trembling in which my kneecaps in particular and the muscles near them danced up and down, quite out of control, though I did my utmost to force them to stop. Eventually the chatter of the audience died and I stumbled out with only two thoughts in my head – that the heating system was working for once so the audience wouldn't freeze, and that the silence of an empty, cold church was quite different from the rustling silence of a warm, full one.

> For ye shall hear how our Heaven King
> Calleth Everyman to a general reckoning:
> Give audience, and hear what he doth say.

So I warned them, those pews full of boys and girls and parents and teachers looking up at me, concentrating. I caught sight of my mother and pointed my last line at her: after all, it was her doing I was up here now spouting this, and I turned away to make my exit, wondering whether the ghosts of long-dead parishioners were listening in the aisles, nodding grave medieval heads at the words of the pulpit's occupant. Back in the vestry I knew such relief as if I had endured ordeals by fire and I could scarcely answer the anxious questions from the rest of the cast. I sat down, blood pulsing through me like falling tears, and I began to feel a glow of satisfaction: my part was done, and it was so good to have finished that I could meet any possibility the world offered.

'Will you hear my words?' Tim asked. Beauty.

He led me into the inner vestry; the only people in there were the Deadly Sins – not properly part of the text, but inventions of Uncle Barry to please three of his first-formers, Jones, Tweazle and Epstein. They were an un-prepossessing trio, dressed in black gowns and green fezzes with red feathers. Even to my untutored eye this did not look medieval.

'Lovers,' said Jones to Epstein in a low voice and they giggled like squeaking chickens gone berserk. I must have blushed enough to gratify them even more than they had hoped.

Tim went through his part and I followed it in the book, sometimes stealing a glance at him, and keeping one ear open for the first-formers' conversation. We were safe; they had returned to their own chatter:

'How does an elephant get up an oak tree?'

'Don't know.'

'Sits on an acorn and waits for it to grow.'

'What's red and comes out of the ground at ninety miles an hour?'

'Don't know.'

'A Rolls Royce carrot.'

Clive Smith came in. On his black tights and leotard a white skeleton had been painted and on his head was a black cowl. His face had been made up like a skull. He smiled and the skull stretched; when he opened his mouth the teeth painted on his lips looked like the hairs of a moustache. 'You're due on in a minute,' he said to Tim.

'God help me!' Tim sounded as if Death had really issued a summons, and giving my hand a squeeze he hurried out. I looked at Clive and the first-formers, but they had noticed nothing: Clive had his back to me; Epstein was telling a joke I had heard years ago at Scouts, and Tweazle, evi-dently the shy one, was pretending he followed it, just like I did at his age.

'Think I'll watch the rest of it,' I said.

'I'll come with you,' Clive answered. He looked strange

as he walked; I suppose I half-expected him to move like a zombie, or dance like a skeleton in a cartoon film, but his legs just went forward as anybody else's, so that the painted bones bent in the wrong places and the ribs moved when he breathed.

Out in the centre of the church was a cylinder of light, and where we were, behind pillars in the south transept, there was half-light and tall, soaring shadows. In the centre Beauty moved and left Everyman; Strength, Five Wits, Discretion, Good Deeds and Knowledge followed. The lights slowly faded and went out. It was all over.

Afterwards it was as if everyone was drunk. Excitement and energy had been let loose; we wanted to shriek with joy, even smash things. Someone made a speech and Uncle Barry thanked us for his present – for my part of which I owed Confession twenty p. Then we were going home, a whole crowd of us, an army of walking scarves and coats and gloves, tramping down through the wood that was made safe because there were so many of us. It was snowing hard, a real blizzard of whirling white flakes that were rapidly obliterating all the dirty prints our feet left. Light from torches made it easy to see the way, and the glimpses I had of the trees showed their knotty roots smoothed out under the snowfall and their trunks silver as on a Christmas card. I lagged behind just to see if I would be afraid now I was on my own; to reassure myself that nothing was going to pounce out of the wood at me.

'Tony.'

My heart thumped violently; Tim had dropped back on purpose. I stretched out my hand and found his. We kissed. I had a fleeting impression that life was *now* and that this was the reason for me being me. The group ahead started to sing *Good King Wenceslas*; it sounded like 'Cooking Wenceslas.' After the first verse nobody remembered the words, so it petered out untunefully, but someone said 'Let's go carol singing,' and there was an excited chorus of agreement.

We followed them up the lane, out of the wood, arms round each other, snow blowing in our faces and finding the gaps between our scarves and ourselves, cold powder on warm throats and necks. We crunched it underfoot and kicked up little showers of it; ahead they were just starting on *The First Nowell*. Tim's torch showed a white crust on all the bars of a gate, and the field beyond was an untouched white sheet. We caught up with them outside my house; they were in the second verse of *Once in Royal David's City*, and my parents, who must have arrived home ages ago, had not yet opened the door. We slipped by, unnoticed; anonymous lovers. We went a very long way round to Tim's house, past Manor Farm. We heard the cows wheeze in their sheds, and a man plodded through the farmyard carrying a lantern made out of an old turnip with a candle inside it. There were the school holidays to come, and Christmas, and Tim. We went into the cowshed and made love on the straw, first love, the first coming ever with another human being, and happiness rose in me, waves and waves of it: life was *now*.

DRAFTS

Adrian Park

Dear Allan,
Thanks for the letter, which reached Glasgow before I did. I think I told you I was going to visit my parents in Manchester on the way home from Toronto. They asked after you; they realised you were someone very special. I enjoyed seeing you again; seeing you happy and settled. Canada seems to be treating you well. I'm not so sure my coming out to stay with you was such a good idea; perhaps it would have been better to make a completely clean break . . . to accept the inevitable. It does no good to cling to the past, no matter how fond the memories. . .

Memories damn it! More like ghosts – unquiet spirits to be exorcised one by one.

. . . Don't misunderstand me. I enjoyed seeing you again – seeing you happy, settled and. . .

Why? Why should I be happy to see that? Damn it! I miss you every day . . . every damned, empty day! And to see you revelling in a new setting. . . Do you have no ghosts of your own? Did I mean so little to you, or can you just shut out the memories?

Dear Allan,
Your letter was waiting for me when I got back from Manchester. It's spring in Glasgow, quite a change from the cold of Toronto. Do you remember the view from the

15

flat? Well, spring always did transform it; the woods in the Kelvin valley are a mass of daffodils and the days have been unseasonably warm. Funny how I always think of Glasgow in terms of woods and sunshine rather than tenements and shipyards. . .

And I think of you. Watching you walk in that sunshine, striding ahead along the Kelvin towpath, your great shaggy mane catching the sun. Gambolling like a big dog, all that restless energy in your shoulders . . . and that open, humorous look, mischievous grin, disarming, gentle eyes.

. . . I think of you often, and I remember us; both of us together. We made a good team, so different but complimentary, fused and ready to take on the world. Those were the happiest three years of my life; I cannot thank you enough for that. . .

Why did they have to end? Why did you have to win that fucking scholarship? And why, why did you have to take it? Hell! The man's gone . . . but the ghost!

. . . The flat is still very much the same, with just the addition of your present, the framed photograph of the 'Queen Mary on sea trials off Arran' on the mantel shelf. . .

Lying toad! Tell him how you smashed it. How you deliberately took it and beat it into fragments with a rolling pin, then cried inconsolably for over an hour. And while you're at it, tell him how you took that hideous ormolu clock he bought you on the Barrows for a joke and attacked it with a hammer. Tell him how you hunted the flat for every photograph of the two of you together and burned them in one desperate auto da fé – one final attempt to erase all trace of his having been there.

. . . The flat seems so empty without you.

Oh God! Don't try that. Blackmail never worked on that selfish bastard while he was here! Why resort to it now? Have you no dignity?

16

Dear Allan,

Thanks for your letter. It was waiting for me when I got back. Thanks for showing me Toronto. It's such a lively, vibrant city; reflecting your nature. You should flourish there. I was delighted to see you still look as unkempt and unbound as I will always remember you. I always needed to work at keeping in trim; with you it just came naturally. . .

Ha! The most vigorous exercise you ever took was picking your nose! . . . No, that isn't strictly true . . .

. . . There was some advertising blurb for the Kelvin Hall proms in the same heap as your letter. Do you remember that time I talked you into going to one? I suppose it was a trade-off; you'd brow-beaten me into going to that UB40 concert. Hmm! Our tastes never did quite meet on that score. I was only thinking the other day about the time we went to watch Partick Thistle. How we nearly froze to death on the terraces – it was the first and only football match I've ever been to. How we got back to the flat to find the gas was off and the place was like a deep freeze! We stayed in bed for thirty-six hours just to keep warm. It was devilish cold that winter, wasn't it? Practise for Toronto I suppose . . .

. . . need I ask who keeps you warm at night there?

. . . Joe and Ross were round for dinner the other evening. They both ask to be remembered to you and send their best wishes. Do you remember that long week-end we spent at Ross's father's cottage on Arisaig? That was a fantastic holiday; just the two of us on an empty coast in late September. We had fires on the beach at night and baked potatoes . . . and made love under the stars. You brought that ridiculous manual with you – laugh! – it almost put me in traction! That was what I loved most about you; your sense of fun was so infectious; you brought people out of themselves . . .

. . . and I wake in the night and imagine you're here, beside me. I reach out and find only emptiness, a space crowded with memories. For such a big, hulking brute you were one of the most gentle, tender men I've ever met. I miss the restrained strength of your touch; your embrace. When we lay together with all passion spent, just the rhythm of your heart in my ear and the syncopation of our breathing for counterpoint, no small talk was necessary as we drifted into sleep; no words of reassurance could express the feelings your arms communicated. It's those little things I miss most, like waking to see you still sound asleep beside me, your hand resting on my stomach. Then there was your coffee . . . dear God! that I will NEVER forget! How anyone can produce such eldritch horror from such simple ingredients I shall never fathom out. You would insist on bringing me a cup of it in bed on Saturday mornings. I'd drink it, express disgust; and you'd apologise in your own inimitable way!

I never was fit for much on Saturdays while you were here!

Dear Allan,

My love has turned to hate in the face of your selfish indifference. That letter was the last straw. You hadn't either the guts or the common decency to tell me to my face while I was in Toronto. You are the most self-centred, egotistical, selfish, unfeeling bastard it's ever been my misfortune to meet. Thank God an ocean separates us; if I never see or hear from you again it will not be too soon! As for that letter, I shall treat it with the contempt it so richly deserves . . .

Frankly, Scarlet my dear, I don't give a damn! . . .

How can I say that? How could I send it? I wish I could learn to hate him. Even psych myself up to hurt him. If I could do that; learn to hate him, perhaps I could forget him.

Some chance!

How do you hate someone like that?

Oh! We could fight like cat and dog; but I could never keep up the pretence of anger, and he found it impossible to bear a grudge. Our fights were a ritual; an excuse for the frantic reconciliation; an anorexic cycle of fasting and gorging.

18

Dear Allan,

Thanks for the letter. The flight back to Britain was very good, though I was jet-lagged for a couple of days. Air Canada have a stylish line in air stewards! Speaking of which, do you remember Carl Evans? Well, I met him at Ringway, of all places – he's on the Manchester-Glasgow shuttle these days, and we came back up here on the same flight. I always did fancy him. Well, he's in Glasgow quite often now, so we're seeing rather a lot of each other . . .

For goodness' sake! How ridiculous can you get? Why drag Carl into it? OK, so we started seeing each other, but two one-night stands and a few beers are hardly the basis for on-going envy!

Why use Carl just to try and make him jealous? What's the point? He's hardly likely to come rushing back on the next flight!

Dear Allan,

Thanks for the letter. It's prompted me to write and thank you for making the trip to Toronto so enjoyable. At first I was shocked that you could not tell me such important news to my face. I mean, I had realised that Vivienne was rather special to you. On consideration thanks for telling me anyhow; it's always difficult to sever yourself from the past, and we did mean . . . still do mean (I hope) a lot to each other. Joe and Ross send their regards. The news took them by surprise, but they are both delighted for you. It's a pity no one from the old gang will be able to come across for the wedding. I only hope this letter gets to you before the big day.

Thanks once again . . . and my fondest best wishes to you both.

Love always,

Frank.

POPPING THE QUESTION

Chris Payne

The only consolation Bernie Pope could find in being a guest at a wedding was that at least *he* wasn't getting hitched. He'd shown up because he couldn't let down his own sister. But, when it had been made clear – over the telephone; what a cowardly way out! – that it might be best if he didn't bring his boyfriend, he'd agreed to come on condition he could stay well in the background, out of the glare of heterosexuals congratulating themselves, as he put it to Mum.

She made a fuss at the time, but mothers have their ways and here was Bernie, trapped in church on the very front bench: Grannie Moffatt at the end, teenage brother Tony, himself, Mum in a lilac outfit, and then Dad who had just accompanied sister Dawn up the aisle. Grannie and Mum had had their hankies out of their new handbags for some time. Endless rows of relatives and friends (which were the more alarming?) were massed behind, as overwhelming to Bernie as the Russian Army in Red Square. From somewhere came the whirr of a video-camera.

Sun shone through the windows high above, and two shafts of it met in the middle of the altar, like spotlights. The vicar asked Dawn and Roger the usual simple questions, and their replies were amplified round the church via a microphone that was hidden somewhere between the three participants, relaying every nuance to the hushed audience. Bernie decided he could annoy his mother afterwards if he commented on the similarity to two lucky contestants and the enthusiastic compère on a game show. Sweet – but meaningless – little triumphs in the face of such a display of strength!

He wasn't usually a spiteful person, and he didn't dislike the human race; indeed, he was fond of all his family, and the groom's folks, though stiff-collared, were not too bad either. The problem was that, like so many gay people, he found weddings and Christmases hard to endure. Both institutions ('Christmas isn't an institution!' Mum asserted) were designed to buoy up the sagging family structure, he thought, and to ignore the very existence of gays. Bernie wasn't just bored and vaguely exasperated, however, as he had been at his cousin Jennifer's marriage to a ginger-haired bank clerk. This time he was angry: first that David hadn't been invited, and that he himself had been forced into the front row against his wishes.

'Where else can you sit?' Dad had asked before they left for the church.

'Doing Mum's dirty work,' he replied.

'Be reasonable, Bernie! It's Dawn's big day, so we all pull together.'

Just as, if he had the energy to mention David and bring it all up later, they'd say, 'Be reasonable: OK, so he wasn't invited, but he wasn't uninvited either. You could have brought him if you'd really wanted to, but where would he have sat? And don't forget,' they'd add, 'Roger's family are old-fashioned . . . and we don't want to upset them.'

'But it doesn't matter whether I'm upset,' he grumbled silently, provoking himself into the same depths of annoyance he'd reached on the train, so that he'd nearly got off and turned back at Peterborough. His lover, David, took a live-and-let-live approach, and kept well away from activities he disapproved of; but Bernie was aggrieved on principle. Which was why he decided he had to do something to keep his self-respect intact, and he knew precisely what that something was. The first person to ask him, as the bride's elder ('But Bernie's still single, you know') brother: when are *you* going to get married? would receive an uncompromising reply – 'I'm gay.' Even if it was Roger or the vicar or Grannie Moffatt. 'They ask an insensitive, nosy question; they get the truth,' he fumed self-righteously.

These thoughts kept him busy till the service was over. He didn't listen to any of it – he was there, that was the main thing: he just stood up and kneeled down when everybody else did. Then the blast of the organ roused him; and the newly-weds were walking arm-in-arm down the aisle . . . The front rows were supposed to follow them. Bernie winked at the video-camera as he passed it, and scrutinised the groom's family walking staidly in front of him. They had one of those funny English names with more syllables in the spelling than in the pronunciation. At the front there were Mother and Father – his hair was terribly short; he'd probably let some old gent loose on it as part of the vital, last-minute preparations of the day before. Then the best man, the younger brother, Charles, older than Bernie's own brother Tony. And Grandfather, the most interesting of them with his bushy white hair and red-veined face: he really looked as if he might horsewhip homosexuals on the steps of his club – when he wasn't whipping the paper-boy down the drive for being late with his Sunday Flesh, that is. The sisters were two of Dawn's bridesmaids, up ahead. Bernie was fairly sure Mother and Father had stopped at four because that's what Her Majesty had done.

Feeling more relaxed now and quite superior, having sorted out Roger's family to his own satisfaction, he stepped into the sunshine. There was a man in a cream jacket at the church gates, running round, organising people for photographs.

O yes, Bernard said to himself, you're one of us.

The man had a deep voice, and told the assembly of wedding personnel to say 'Holidays!'

'Who's he?' Bernie asked Tony.

'Works with Dad.' At which point it was Bernie's turn to join the ever-changing group before the camera. On closer inspection the photographer proved to be tanned and greying at the temples. Fifties, looks thirties, Bernie decided.

'. . . And if you'll stand there . . . Smashing!' The man took him by the wrist and put him in place like a vase of flowers. Bernie stood deliberately staring at the man, not at the camera.

'Someone's not looking at the birdie,' the photographer wheedled. 'That's better. Say "Holidays!" everybody.' Whirr. Whirr. He wore a silver ring on his little finger.

Grandfather Horsewhip and Grannie Moffatt were next to join the happy group – one on either side – and as the photographer charmed Grannie into position, Bernie helped by doing the same to the outraged old man. But when Mum coaxed Tony into the frame, Bernie was forced to stifle a strong urge to laugh, because Dad's workmate was taking such trouble over that young man, patting his arms, holding his wrists, standing him up straight and telling him to make sure he showed his teeth. Lovely teeth! Then he patted him all over again. To think of poor Dawn, waiting centre-shot, whilst a homosexual fondled her little brother right under her nose! Tony turned and winked at Bernie, for he wasn't as innocent as he looked. So, when the pictures came out, Mum would be delighted to see (apart from the one where he was tapping his nose with his forefinger) Bernie laughing uproariously and looking as though nobody enjoyed the wedding as much as he did.

Bernie looked across at the wolf in sheep's clothing chatting to Dad about cameras, and Auntie Pam came over for a word. He immediately hoped she'd be the one to ask the question; anyway, Dad's family were generally quite sensible, so she probably wouldn't scream or faint when he told her. But Auntie Pam confined herself chiefly to Dawn's dress, and the only question she asked Bernie was about the weather in London, obviously sure that nowhere in the world could be sunnier than the church and its environs at that particular moment. Soon she rushed off to discuss the wedding dress with someone who appreciated it better.

Bernie drew a long breath of boredom and frustration,

and reckoned it was time he gave his sister a chance to thank him for being so well-behaved. She and Roger were back on the church steps talking to the vicar – who definitely caught Bernie's eye as he approached. *Not another!*

In fact he wasn't the vicar but an old friend of Roger's, his university chaplain. He had a lingering handshake, and soon showed a keen interest in Bernie's education. Dawn drifted over to another group, no doubt saving her expressions of gratitude to her brother till much later, after he had completed the whole day without trouble. Roger slipped after her as quickly as possible – perhaps it wasn't good form for the groom to be seen deep in conversation with two homosexuals straight after the ceremony, or perhaps he had no idea he was in such a position, and simply wanted to be as close to his new wife as he could.

The chaplain spoke with wide knowledge of education, and studied Bernie's face as he spoke. The man possessed a lively smile and a mischievous manner. After a few minutes it turned out that the two of them had a mutual acquaintance, a lecturer whom Bernie had always assumed to be gay, and a little while after that, the chaplain said confidentially, 'Hear you're not married yourself. Nor me.' Then he added, 'But you've more alternatives than I had, I'm sure.' At this point Mum came over to thank him for performing so well: we could hear every word, blah, blah! Bernie smirked at her. She was glad he was enjoying the wedding.

A fleet of white-ribboned limousines and an assortment of private cars took the whole party to the hotel where Dad had hired a banqueting suite. Altogether, it must have cost enough to keep a gay man in pet food for the whole of his adult life. Bernie was privileged to be in the second Daimler, sitting opposite Grannie M. He did hope she wouldn't pop the question during the journey because, if she did, two uncles, an aunt and a nine-year-old cousin would unavoidably hear the frank reply. On reflection, Grannie M. was leading his betting, because he knew she had a firm opinion of what was good for everyone, and used subtle comments such as, 'You're twenty-five and still single,

24

Bernard.' In that case it would serve her right. Also he'd heard her confide once to Mum, when the subject came up on television, that she'd never met any of these 'theatricals', and he rather fancied introducing her to one.

In the event, her stomach rumbled very loudly and they all passed the journey joking about it. For an elderly lady, she had an excellent sense of humour and an even better appetite.

There was white wine served on the lawn before the meal began, and more photos. Bernie mused over how to tell Dad about his workmate; then he wondered how to make the most of telling Mum about the chaplain. Grannie Moffatt kept bobbing in and out of the pictures. Bernie had set his sights on her and several times he had to steel himself in preparation . . . hold your breath . . . here it comes . . . but the moment passed, and after a quarter of an hour he grew tired of waiting. He decided he'd give Dawn and Roger the pleasure again. He wasn't sure how much Roger knew about him, but he suspected he'd been told and had ignored the fact ever since. He certainly wasn't the type to ask nosy questions, nor were any of his family – that was why bringing David would surely have passed off without embarrassment. Homosexuality was the kind of subject Roger's people just did not speak about, even though Father must have encountered it in the Navy, and Roger had asked a man who hardly pretended to be other than gay to officiate at his marriage.

Bernie generously told the newly-weds how good they looked together, and kissed his sister's cheek. He wondered whether she'd ask after David – she usually did. But no, no mention. Bernie began to be angry again. Just because of Roger, she wasn't asking. They'd been married half an hour, and she was already co-operating in his family's true-blue, establishment-censorship tactics. He left her to it.

'Bernard, come and meet Roger's family,' said Mum as he passed. No escape. He had to shake hands with Father, Mother, Charles and Grandfather. It felt like a job interview, but Mum seemed to have worked out how to talk to

25

them and she was getting along famously with the pop-eyed old man.

The others had moved on and only Charles was left. He and Bernie found they had absolutely nothing to say. They shuffled. Each second of silence made the embarrassment more pronounced, but Charles's brand of stiff-upper-lip reserve, old before his time, left Bernie quite inadequate. Suddenly a spark lit up in Charles's face. He had thought of something convivial to say.

'How about you? Got any plans for marrying?'

Bernie had told himself what the answer would be so many times, always imagining his triumph as his Gran or some minor uncle or other distant relative heard the reply.

Momentum carried him on. 'No, I'm gay,' he said, expressionlessly, before he had a chance to recover from the surprise. To his own ears it sounded appallingly aggressive. All Roger's family had been a hundred to one shots because they were basically too polite, too nice to ask such a question, and now Bernie looked at the stricken young man and wished he'd said something harmless, however dishonest.

'Good God, you're not serious!'

Make a fool of himself now by pretending he wasn't serious? He looked blankly at Charles, and said, 'They're going indoors.'

Bernie had been looking forward to the meal, gastric juices gurgling in anticipation of the brightest spot of the whole day, but suddenly he didn't want any food. Fortunately the placings meant that Charles and he couldn't see each other, but Bernie still sat miserably regretting his words, indeed wishing he'd had it in him to have found an excuse not to have come at all. That would have been true courage, yes, rather than spiteful, childish attempts to revenge himself while he was here. He realised, too, that it wouldn't have been any better to have told Grannie Moffatt – there she was two seats away, tucking into her roast beef as if the life of the flowers on her wedding hat depended on it; but he'd have spoiled it for her. He felt as angry with himself as he had with Mum earlier.

This was the reality of weddings for gay people, Bernie thought, if they were stupid enough to attend them, or unless they were mature enough not to be bothered. Perhaps the photographer didn't consider weddings as an insult because he could go home to his lover and laugh about them. That was another thing Bernie debated with himself; just because a gay man was camp and fifty, he was automatically treated as a joke. That, Bernie told himself, is how far you've progressed with the help of your liberated life in London, mate. You stupid pillock!

When the sherry trifle was served Bernie offered his portion to his little cousin (who accepted greedily and began to taunt her brother with it) and found himself wondering whether Charles would keep the information quiet: it could be all the way round the table. He stood, murmured in Dad's ear that he wanted some fresh air, and walked out onto the lawn. Beyond a shaped hedge was a gravel walk to a lily-pond and a fountain that had a statue of a curly-haired boy, semi-naked and on one leg, gargling water out of his mouth. Facing this soothing display was a bench, which Bernie was glad to sit on.

He thought of David, and for the first time admitted to himself that his lover would not have come at any price. This fact had been kept to one side to let the anger through, but now Bernie's anger was directed inwards. He knew David's laughter wouldn't be malicious but he felt so sick at what he'd done that he decided not to tell him. At this moment he realised somebody was approaching.

What happened next seemed like slow motion when he remembered it later, and the babble of the fountain, when he recalled it, much louder. As he turned, Charles slumped to his knees on the grass. 'I saw you walk out,' Charles said. 'I thought . . . I thought . . . I was the only one.'

'The only . . . ? We're everywhere today . . . You were well disguised though!'

'Yes.'

'We can talk afterwards, when all this nonsense is over.' He squeezed Charles's hand, then caught a movement out of the corner of his eye. 'Tony! Come here!' he shouted. 'What are you skulking about like that for?'

'Mum sent me to find out how you are,' Tony said, surveying them. 'Looks as if you're doing all right to me.' Charles was still on his knees. 'Shall I tell her his folks'll be paying for this one?'

A RIGHT SHOWER

Chris McVey

The man pressed on the bench with both hands to hoist himself up, his breathing easier now. Then he waddled over to the inclining-board and stood nodding with approbation over the boy's sit-ups. Time after time the luxuriant ash-blond head sprang up to caress the brown young knees. As it arched back to the bottom of the board, the shapely singlet fell back too, exposing the hard ridges of muscle above the shiny shorts. His eyes were closed, the long lashes tight in concentration.

The man began to perspire again. 'Hard work, eh?' he offered, a fellow athlete.

'No, not really. Not for me it isn't.' The long lashes lifted with a hint of disdain, but the blue of his eyes and the white of his teeth couldn't resist a smile. He flattened back to rest, blowing the blond flick from his face with practised ease.

The man breathed out through pursed lips as he strained to lean down. 'No, no,' he quickly conceded, his plump fingers professionally testing the boy's abdominal muscles. 'No, you're not in bad shape at all, for a beginner.' He allowed himself a painful glance at his own amorphous mass. 'I was this shape when I was your age!' The quip was based upon fact and produced no response beside his own snicker of shame. To appease the silence, he added, 'I need all the exercise I can get.'

The boy cast his blue gaze across the bulging expanse of track-suit. 'Yes, too right,' he candidly agreed.

'I'm in a sedentary occupation,' the man explained,

lowering his bulk on to the neighbouring inclining-board and ignoring its wheezing protest. 'Sit on my arse all day driving a taxi. Should be at it now, by rights.' He glanced at his action-man digital watch, shifted his weight a little, but stayed where he was.

His young companion arranged himself comfortably on the board, allowing the strap across his feet to take the burden of his weight, hands behind his head. Newton's law of gravity arranged the bottom of his singlet across his chest. 'A cab-driver, eh?' He gave his blond flick another blow, like an absent-minded kiss. 'An interesting job, so I've heard – meeting people.'

The man warmed to his topic. One thing about work, it was something to talk about; it created openings. An ill wind. 'Oh, I meet people, all right! Pop stars and civic dignitaries . . . weirdoes, mostly.' He sniggered meaningfully and rested a fat hand casually on the boy's hard belly. 'Yes, nice and flat, that.' He allowed his impudent fingers to probe tentatively. 'Concave almost. I hope you do plenty of back exercises.'

The boy came suddenly bolt upright, a look of concern in his child's face. 'Should I do back exercises, then?'

The man permitted his trembling hand, which he had lifted in false alarm, to scurry down for another legitimate exploration. 'Oh, yes, indeed!' he said. 'What I don't know about the workings of the male physique . . . Yes, you must exercise the back to be nice and concave in front.' With fresh confidence, his curious fingers burrowed beneath the elastic of the shorts, discovering, to their delight, a furrow of soft down.

'But I don't know any back exercises,' the boy pouted. It wasn't fair.

The fat stranger said, 'I could show you some, if you like.' Altruism had triumphed.

'Oh, cheers! Would you?' The innocent youth was all hope, gratitude and enthusiasm. 'I mean, if you've got the time.'

The man recalled his reluctant hand to glance anxiously at his watch. 'Yes, the time factor,' he mused aloud. 'Yes, time's money all right, to coin a phrase. All the same, I like

30

to encourage manly pursuits. I should be out there plying for trade but still . . . all work and no play. . . and you need a partner for what I'd like you to do.' Restlessly, he consulted his watch again and glanced around the gym. 'One good thing,' he continued in a hoarse undertone, 'it's nice and quiet this time of the day. The showers'll be empty. I look forward to the shower.' He jogged a moment, flabbily, on the spot, to relieve some nagging tension. 'Come with me,' he whispered, lifting the boy by his armpits, 'over to the bench.' He guided him across the floor, his damp, chubby hands owning the slender waist.

'Good lad. Now lie face down across the bench. That's it. Get your . . . groin . . . clear of the edge. Well done! Don't worry, you won't fall off. You'll be safe with me sitting on your legs.' The big man straddled the smooth young legs, tight against the short, shiny shorts, his large hands resting hot upon the resilient buttocks. He took a deep breath to calm his voice. 'Now, with your hands behind your head, go right down until your head touches the floor. That's it. Now . . . return to the starting position. Oh, very good! And again. Keep going until I tell you to stop.'

The boy continued the exercise, his movements graceful and effortless.

'OK, stop now. Good boy, well done! What do you feel now?'

'Your hands on my bottom,' the boy truthfully replied.

'Exactly!' said his mentor, loudly and after only the slightest hesitation. 'Well done, quite right. When you feel the buttocks twitch against the hands, you've come up nice and straight.' Somehow, the definite article rendered the intimacy appropriately objective. 'You should also feel the back muscles tightening,' he added. 'Carry on, then.'

The boy obeyed, the blond top bobbing rhythmically, the firm bottom twitching in athletic counterpoint, as the man's talk got back to his work.

'Yes, all kinds I come across. Meet all sorts I do, in the taxi-ing game. Politicians, the lot.' He guffawed weakly. 'Picked up a right crowd the other night. All hips and limp wrists waving about the cab.'

'What . . . politicians?' The boy's body stiffened with

surprise and came to a sudden halt, only to be set in motion again by a sharp tap on the head from the teacher.

'Keep going, lad; let's feel that twitch. No, not politicians, although I don't know, they might've been Liberals. I picked 'em up in the taxi – outside that weird club. The one with the Greek name, you know.'

'Oh, yes, too right.' The boy's backside contracted correctly as his head bobbed up to speak.

'What?' The man's fat hands moistened against the shiny little shorts and he drew a shallow breath. 'You know it, then, that club?' His uncertain laugh was just audible. 'You haven't been in there, surely?'

'No, never. Have you?'

'*Me*?' He laughed louder now, at the unthinkable. 'No, not *in* there, no!' How hot it was, not even doing anything, just pressing astride a thrashing, tirelessly energetic boy! A shower would be a welcome relief. 'Yes, all cropped haircuts and toothbrush moustaches they were, this lot. Bunches of keys with secret meanings. Get you, dear, she this and she that.' He made an indignant, retching sound. 'All blokes, of course. Makes you want to puke. It's all legal nowadays, naturally.'

'Naturally,' the boy agreed, not sounding in the least breathless.

The shiny shorts felt quite damp and slippery now under his sweating hands. 'Kinky leather pants. Corporal punishment's too good for 'em in my view; stricter penalties, I'd recommend.' He prised his hand away, clenched his fist and looked aggressively at his watch. 'OK,' he told his pupil, with a playful slap. 'That'll do. Good boy. How do you feel?'

'I feel a bit stiff, actually,' the boy confessed, and jumped up to touch his toes, loosening up. The man joined him.

'Oh, you'll be stiff by now, all right,' he sympathised. 'I'm pretty stiff myself.' He stood erect, shoulders back, an athletic pear. 'Still . . . nothing a good, hot shower can't sort out.' His eyes darted around the empty gym. 'Be ready for a shower yourself by the time you've finished.'

The boy smiled and stretched, tugging his little shorts up his smooth thighs. 'A shower, oh, yes,' he agreed, with en-

32

thusiasm. 'Too right.' He became aware of some doughy mass patting his bottom.

'Mind you,' the man observed diagnostically, 'you want to keep nice and taut down here.' He inhaled deeply. 'The buttocks, I mean. Oh, they're nice and trim as they are, I'll grant you; but you want to keep it that way. Do plenty of squats, I should.'

'Squats?' The boy was mystified. 'What's squats?'

The self-appointed coach looked askance. 'What, you don't do squats?' It was inconceivable. 'You must do some squats. Keep the buttocks convex. Concave here. . .' His palm pressed against the firm young abdomen, the podgy fingers spreading wide. 'And convex here.' He illustrated the point with his other hand, tracing the contour of youthful bottom to where the shorts ended. 'Tell you what,' he gasped, 'I'll make time to show you, as it's important.' Wrenching his hands away, he shambled off to fetch a steel bar from the wall-rack. Returning, he set the bar across his shoulders to demonstrate. Coming up strenuously the third or fourth time, he ground to a breathless halt and handed over the bar. 'Now your turn,' he said. His young protégé began to imitate the exercise. 'Good boy, yes. Keep the back nice and straight, though.'

The man flexed his ample jowls and quivered with masculine appreciation. But it was time now for more talk, and he resumed his monologue of work experience. 'As I was saying,' he rambled on, 'a right shower of nancy boys, this gang of passengers were. Still, mustn't be too choosy nowadays, I suppose. Got to earn a crust. Time's money, as I say.' He glanced at his watch. 'Yes, finish these few squats, a nice, long shower and back to the grindstone. . . No, keep your . . . keep the back straight. Come on, straight, I said.' With apparent impatience, he closed in from behind, the two bodies touching, and reached round to grasp the hard chest muscles. 'That's it, that's better,' he encouraged. 'I'll stay behind you and keep you straight. Yes, that's much better.' Rhythmically now, the two contrasting bodies rose and fell in unison as the man went on. 'Oh, yes, a right bevy of poufters, they were. Bloody shirt-lifters, I call 'em. Make you want to throw up, don't they?'

33

He stopped talking. Only his desperate panting and crack-ing knee-joints broke the heavy silence. 'Well, don't they make you sick?' he insisted. 'What do you think of them funny people, then?'

The boy hesitated a moment. 'Oh . . . oh, yes, too right.' After another brief pause, he added, 'I hear they're OK to talk to, though.'

'Oh, to talk to, yes, to talk to. You're broad-minded, I see. I'm broad-minded myself, of course. I'm glad you're a broad-minded kid. Phew! Be red hot, the water in the showers. Always is this time of day, when it's nice and quiet.' In order to glance at his watch, he tore his shaking hand from the tantalising chest muscles, then let it fly in-voluntarily back again. 'Only a youngster, one of these pansy boys was,' he went on. 'A young kid about your age, I'd say. How old are you?'

'Eighteen. Today. It's my birthday.'

The man nearly lost his precarious balance with the ex-citement. 'Eighteen today? I wish I'd known. I'd've got you a present. I'd like nothing better than to give you one. Still, perhaps I'll think of something.' He regained his com-posure and continued. 'Yes, a good-looking kid he was, too, apart from. . . Quite like you, really. I nearly said to him: What's a nice kid like you. . . ?'

He stopped quite suddenly, exhausted at last. 'OK, that'll do the trick. Good lad, well done! Call it a day, eh? Time's getting on. Time's money. Time for a shower, though. Phew!' He wiped his brow. 'Always make time for a shower. How do you feel?'

The boy put his hands behind his ash-blond head and tensed every supple sinew. 'Pretty stiff, really,' he an-swered. His blue eyes were shining. The man's eyes peered into them, steely and narrow.

'Me, too,' he murmured thickly. 'Stiff as a poker, I am. Soon be in the showers, though, the pair of us. You'll be well ready for the nice, empty, red-hot shower, I'll bet . . . eh?'

The young boy, just eighteen, stretched his smooth arms high above his lovely ash-blond head. 'Too right,' he yawned. Crooking his arms, he flexed the hard, young biceps. He stood, nice and straight, a moment; then twisted his willowy trunk from side to side, unconsciously but magnificently stretching the short, shiny shorts and the unnecessarily flattering singlet. 'First thing I'll do. Finish off with a good jog home and straight into the shower. Too right.'

The bulging mass of the fat man's track-suit subsided visibly and his capacious jowls sagged. He lowered his pendulous buttocks wearily onto the bench and gaped, open-mouthed, at the empty inclining-board. What began as a nervous titter ended more like a pathetic sob. 'Oh . . . oh, yes,' he sighed. 'When you get home. Yes, a good idea. I wish I'd thought of it. *Too* right.' He looked again at his watch.

RIOT

Paul Gurney

Well when I heard about the riot when they shot that woman I thought brilliant I hope they kill every fucking fascist pig in London and about time too and I hopped skipped jumped danced around as if it was *Guess Who's Coming To Dinner* and instead of Sidney Poitier tho' that would've been just fine that bloke from Loose Ends you know the one I mean was coming to dinner, which incidentally I was just cooking, and since you ask it was an organic vegan pot-pourri, truly a culinary Pandora's Box; anyway I was soaking the seaweed and playfully slashing at the smoked tofu like it was a fascist's face while someone in the other room chased police radio broadcasts when a new feeling rose up in me, felt like it began around my knees, then through my loins – groin – thighs, then my trunk – it was a long time in my trunk – up through my heart and lungs soft warm rolling against my ribs ENT ear nose throat getting to the eyes about the same time as it reached the back of my mind, then the front, and anyway I could tell this feeling was two feelings mixed up but it was definitely one feeling which was kinda funny 'cos the two bits were excitement and jealousy, I mean I was *so* excited I think 'cos I was a bit frightened; God! This was better than a by-election and I was jealous 'cos I felt left out and not just 'cos it was a mile away and it was blocked off but jealous 'cos my boyfriend, my lovely boyfriend, was there in the thick of the terror mob go-on-rampage-orgy-of-looting-lawlessness I just *knew* he was 'cos he's so brave and strong and he lives with Christina who just doesn't care and is wilfully outrageous and I bet he got a stack system and maybe he'll get me a duvet and then he'd stay round here more but mainly I was jealous 'cos he was rioting with his New Man who I haven't met yet tho' it'll be really nice when we do 'cos he'll be really nice 'cos he *is* really nice and I'll be really nice 'cos I *am* really and it'll be *OK* 'cos it'll *have* to be 'cos it *ought* to be but boy am I jealous 'cos maybe he's braver than me or if he isn't he's being looked after by my lovely boyfriend and the way he looks after me when we bunk the tube or when we nick drinks at the Jungle oh it's NOT FAIR, oh ME ME ME! I wish he'd just call me up, this lovely boyfriend of mine, and say hey kid you wanna come rioting? (breathlessly) Yes? OK, pick you up about seven thirty, OK? And I'd throw on my best situationalist togs and some Eau Sauvage and lip-salve and bounce out the door walking on air like that old K-Skips advert before your time you say you filthy liar and bathed in the warm flattering Molotov half-light I'd smile carefree and whisper a soft 'Anarchy' in his ear and I'd be so brave, with him I'm never afraid . . . but here I am with News at Ten and, ah le Piat d'Or and a post-structuralist ratatouille, again . . . oh, let them eat cake!

PHONE CALLS FROM FATHER

Wyl Lawrence

'Yes, Father.' Ian shook his head.
  'No, Father.' He nodded.
  'Honestly, Father, what *do* you think I am?'

Best not answer that, dear, or we'll be here all night.

His eyes scanned the ceiling.
  'Yes, I know it's a good job and that I should look after it. . . Yes, I also know that I'm lucky to have one and I *do* realise that they're not easy to get these days.'

Oh, for Christ's sake, George! Give us a break!

'No, Father, I've not been "fooling around" as you so quaintly put it.'

Well, not in the way you mean, honey.

'And I can assure you I have absolutely *no* intention of getting any young lady, or old one for that matter, into any sort of trouble.'
  The first honest statement of the last ten minutes, and probably its true significance would be totally lost on George.
  'No, there aren't any particular girlfriends about at the moment.' *Nor will there ever be, petal.* 'And I've certainly no plans to start a family, so you've no need to rush out and

start knitting matinée jackets.' Ian smiled, picturing his sixty-year-old Dad hamfistedly attempting to master this difficult art. 'No, I was being facetious. It was meant to be a joke. Good grief, Father, have you lost your sense of humour?'

Obviously.

'OK, OK, forget it. If it makes you feel any better . . . I'm sorry.'

For God's sake, man, let the matter alone! I know that you can't tell a dropped stitch from a dropped aitch, but that's not quite the case for all of us, dearest.

'Right then, Father . . . Yes . . . Take care . . . Yes, I'll wait in next Thursday for you to phone.'

And this time please don't ring till Crossroads has finished.

'I will . . . You look after yourself; don't go straining your back in that garden . . . Yes, I know your runner beans are the best for miles around – you told me.'

About two billion times already.

'OK. Be good. Give my regards to anyone who asks.' *Not that they will.* 'Yes, tell them I'll be home soon.' *So then they can slag me and give everyone else a chance of a rest.* 'No, I won't . . . Yes, Father. Bye! Goodbye!'

And good riddance.

Ian replaced the receiver, exhaled deeply, and sank back into the cushions.

'And there we had the latest gripping episode of "Suburbia: My Part In Its Horticulture" from George Edward Cadwallader Hot-Water-Bottle Peanut-Brain Hoskin, coming specially for you live from his very own simulated leather and plastic pot-planted front parlour, somewhere in the depths of scintillating downtown Milton Keynes.'

'You don't come from Milton Keynes.'

I give up.

'Lord above, Kelvin! You're getting as bad as pater der-angus! No, I don't come from Milton Keynes. *Nobody* comes from Milton sodding Keynes. Have you ever seen it? It functions along the same lines as an elephants' graveyard. People only go there to die or raid the ivory.' Realising he'd wrongly channelled his frustration onto his lover, Ian stretched out a hand. 'I'm sorry, I didn't mean to bite your head off.' He gave Kelvin a peck on the cheek. 'You know I come from Bristol. Sunny Avonmouth, hub of the civilised universe. Alternative capital of the Western World. Throbbing metropolis of teeming night life. Home of high technology. Heart of the –'

'I think I get your drift.'

'Oh, I'm sorry, Kelv! I don't mean to be sarcastic – it's just that old George Edward gets to me after a while. It's the same cracked seventy-eight he plays week in, week out, world without end Amen. I can recite the conversation we're going to have before it even starts.'

'Is it really that bad?'

'Worse.' Ian smiled and shook his head in resignation. 'I suppose the old bugger's only trying to show some concern, but I do wish he'd find a way to express it other than trying to tell me how to run my life. It's not as if he's the remotest idea of what it's all about, let alone what I'm like now. Honestly, I swear he still thinks of me as the fresh-faced young innocent who scuttled off to college nearly a decade ago. God, is it *that* long? Oh, I feel old!'

'Has anyone ever told you you're an idiot?'

'Frequently, my dear, frequently. And frankly, I don't give a damn.'

'Eat your heart out, Clark Gable . . . and about the only thing you and he have in common is that *your* ears stick out too.'

'Thank you for those few kind words, and who's rattled your cage?'

'My lover, who's one hundred and fifty per cent certifiable, but he loves me.'

'You should be so lucky!'

'Oh, I am!'

They held each other close for a moment.

'Seriously,' Kelvin said, pulling away from Ian, 'don't you think it's about time you told your old man the truth? My parents accept us and they're hardly the epitome of middle-class liberalism, are they? I don't want to press the point, but –'

'Oh yeah?'

'No, I don't.' Kelvin's voice was a little more forceful. 'But I thought it might help clear the air a bit, and, if nothing else, telling him would relieve the pressures of Thursday evenings.'

'Have you tried talking to my father?' Ian demanded, his voice rising half an octave in agitation. 'It's like trying to compete with the speaking clock! The only difference is that with TIM, at least you get the pips as a respite. Once he starts there's no stopping him! He just engages automatic pilot, slips into over-drive and careers on, hell-for-leather along some predestined path as if there's no tomorrow. Come rain or storm, nothing's going to stop him, and I mean *nothing*!'

'Like father, like son,' Kelvin observed, quietly.

'First he always asks why I've "put on that stupid voice." I begin to tell him that possibly my accent's changed because I've been away from home so long, but I seldom get past the first few syllables before I'm treated to several pages from *The Embalmer's Express*. An intricate itinerary of who's died recently, who's dying, and who ought to have dropped dead. Then, without pausing for breath, let alone grief, I'm subjected to an oration on how long we've all got on this earth and how by rights his time will be up soon. Not that he'll be sad to go, because he'll be happy once more with Elizabeth, my mother. Then he's off again at full pelt, telling me where the insurance policies are and who's to come back to the house after the burial, etcetera. All good cheering stuff! Next, everybody's minor indiscretions are microscopically analysed for my delectation. Not that

I'm particularly interested in knowing who's pregnant, who's married, divorced or living in sin, or who's responsible for disembowelling Mrs Somebody-or-other's ginger tom under the wheels of their car.'

Ian lit two cigarettes and passed one to Kelvin before continuing.

'Having completed this diary of death and despondency, G.E. then turns his tack to me.' He sighed. 'You'd swear to hear him talk that I'd not eaten a square meal in a month of Sundays, and that I was totally incapable of boiling an egg!'

'But you are.'

'That is beside the point! And anyway, how's he to know, never having seen my culinary limitations put to the test?'

'Intuition?'

'Kelvin, I get the distinct impression you're losing interest in what I'm saying! If that's the case, I'm sure I can find better things to do than boring you to distraction.'

'No. No. I'm not bored,' Kelvin said. 'It's fascinating to see you like this, so het up over a phone call! Does your father always have this effect on you?'

'Why do you think I tell him to phone on Thursdays?'

'Because I'm usually at work till late?'

'Precisely.' Ian drew on his cigarette. 'By the time you're back, I've pretty well calmed down. . . Oh, I don't know; it's a bloody farce really! I just let him get to me. Maybe it's some sort of guilt complex or social conditioning, but. . . No, I don't have an answer. I make the effort . . . it's *so* hard at times! I still write once a week, every Wednesday, at work.'

'I didn't think you bothered any more.'

Ian laughed. 'The old sod receives pages of my purple prosody each Friday morning. It's the only way I get to tell him the news. Mind you, it's dressed up a bit to suit his interpretations of what I'm expected to be as a "responsible young man." '

'I can imagine.'

'Mm . . . for example, before I met you, Fridays I'd go for a drink with the boys. Saturdays I'd go for a dance with the girls, which, up to a point is the truth, except that the girls of Saturday night were almost invariably the boys of Friday night.'

He gave a sheepish grin and a little shrug.

Kelvin laughed. 'The semantics of diplomacy.'

'Yes.'

'Plus the dreaded sin of omission.'

'Exactly.' Ian took a final drag on his cigarette and put it out. 'I suppose it's the same for most of us – there's never really an end to coming out, is there? You've always got to meet new people, and one way or another they find out. I've never lied about my sexuality; it's just that I don't want to make it into an issue. If people ask, I tell them the truth. Father's never asked. All my friends know – they guessed at work, so I confirmed it; and the guys down at the gym weren't slow in putting two and two together when they realised I was living with Geoffrey.'

Kelvin pretended to spit at the mention of Ian's ex-affair.

'Oh, I've thought of telling him several times, but come the crunch, I've always allowed myself to be swept along by the tide of his verbosity. That's where I get it from.'

'What?'

'The ability to waffle for ages without actually saying very much. Father's the same, only now he's stuck in a groove, so all you ever get is instant replay, time after time.'

'Come on! He's not *that* bad!'

'Before Mother died,' Ian said, 'it used to be all-out open warfare, loaded armchairs and all that. After she'd gone a strained peace evolved, mainly I think because we both realised that there was no one else in the family to turn to. Father got post-interment depression along the lines of "Why wasn't it me?" and "Life's not worth living," so I kept an eye on him – filial duty I suspect. On his part he began this weekly ritual and it's continued ever since. I've persuaded myself that he needs it more than me, but deep down inside, I know that if for some reason he stopped phoning, I'd soon be down there to find out why.'

Kelvin began to realise what lay behind it all. 'Do you need your father's approval?'

'No,' Ian replied, a little too quickly.

Kelvin nailed home his point. 'So why don't you just tell him then, and get it off your chest? You've nothing to lose if that's the case, and you gain a clear conscience. Every way a winner.'

'You don't know my father!' Ian protested.

'No, and I never will if you keep on denying my existence.'

'I mean, last time I saw him, his main obsession was to rebuke me for having my ear pierced. Now do you genuinely see that as a situation conducive to coming out? Yes, Father, isn't it barbaric having bits of metal skewered through my flesh? I quite agree, and yes of course I'll wear an armband in memory of Mrs Pink-Antimacassar's canary's sad demise in the jaws of a rabid sabre-tooth spaniel. Oh, and by the way, Father, your son's a screaming queen who goes around permitting other perverts to defile his beautiful body. Christ! How quickly do you think I could build a fall-out shelter? It wouldn't be fast enough to avoid an apocalyptic assault and a probably fatal coronary! No, Kelvin, I think it best to let sleeping Dads lie. Keep up the pretence and allow him to labour under his own sweet delusions. If, and I said *if*, I do in some way need his approval, I sure as hell can't see me getting it by confirming that he'll never be a grandfather.'

'I don't know,' Kelvin said. 'It may help to pave the way to a better mutual understanding; something which doesn't exist at the moment.'

'Oh, come on! Forget it! It's your first Thursday off in ages. Let's go to the pub. I hear they've got a drag act on that's supposed to be quite good.'

'Two six nine double seven. . . Yes, Father. . . No, Father, this *is* my proper accent. I've been living in the Midlands for six years now. . . Yes, it might sound funny to you, but they all talk like this up here.'

Ian shot Kelvin an I-told-you-so look and tried to pick up the threads of the conversation. It had got to the obituary column.

'He's dead? Well I. . . Two hundred and fifty thousand!

44

Where'd he get all that from? . . . Oh, really? . . . Well, I never . . . I don't believe it! No, not you, Father: it. I don't believe *it*!'

Are you going deaf as well as daft, you old fool?

'No. I didn't say anything. We must have a crossed line.' He stared helplessly at Kelvin, who encouraged him with a smile and a wink. 'They haven't? And what did the vicar have to say about *that*?'

Kelvin was beginning to suspect that Ian was deliberately prompting the trivia. 'Go on,' he urged. 'Tell him. You promised.'

'Saturday night,' Ian hissed, 'when I was totally ratted and didn't know anything about it till Sunday afternoon. . . No, nothing, Father.'

Kelvin's eyes narrowed. 'Go on,' he mouthed.

'Father,' Ian said, 'Father, listen. I've got something to tell you. . . No, it won't wait till my letter. I want you to hear this *now*. . . Listen . . . look, it's important. . . Yes, a damn sight more important than your bloody roses. . . Yes, I'm sorry I swore, but it's important and I don't know where to start . . . I know the beginning's the most logical place, and I'd start there if only I knew where it was. . . No, I wasn't being sarcastic. . . Oh, for crying out loud, Father! Here's me trying to tell you probably the single most important thing of my life, and you're prattling on about some idiot's parsnips being bigger than yours!'

It's not the size; it's what you do with it.

'I'll bet they don't taste as good as yours . . . No.'

Oh, my God! Listen to me this once, you meandering moron!

'Father, are you listening? Well, you know how I always said that I'd get married when the time was right? Yes, well, I don't think the time will ever be right. For me to marry . . . a girl, I mean. I guess what I'm trying to tell you is that. . .' He took a deep breath. 'I'm trying to tell you I'm gay.'

45

He cringed in expectation.
'Father, are you still there?'

Don't die on me, you old gargoyle! I look bog awful in black.

The two lovers exchanged glances. Ian shook the receiver.
'Father? Father!'

Thank God for that!

'What exactly do you mean? What do you mean you already knew?' Ian's face registered his indignation. 'Who told you?' he shrieked. 'When? . . . and you didn't think it nice to let me in on this? What do you mean, you didn't know how to broach it? . . . Fucking hell, Father. . . Hang on a minute, I need a cigarette.'
Kelvin lit one for him.
'Listen. . . Yes, of course I'm all right! . . . I'm not upset that you didn't tell me. You've told me now; that's all that matters. . . No, I haven't got a cold; I'm sniffing for other reasons. . . . No, it's definitely not that either! . . . Look, listen, what are you doing this week-end? . . . Why? . . . Because I'd like you to come up for a few days. Your garden will have to do without you for a bit . . . I'd like you to come up because there's someone rather special that I'd like you to meet.' He drew Kelvin towards him. 'Yes, Father, someone *very* special. His name is Kelvin, and, yes, before you ask, he *has* got a good job. . .'

TOMBOY

James Macveigh

Ah, those days! The first time Marcel ever saw her he had mistaken Isabel for a boy, and he wondered now if that had added to the attraction. As his evening train slipped through endless vineyards, sometimes passing a road the colour of pastry, he let himself drift back through the years until there he was, rattling ice in his glass again behind Boyer's villa at Cap Ferrat. She came out of the trees on the far side of the pool, wearing only a shirt and the briefest of shorts. Long, golden legs. Scratched knees. Hair like unruly straw and a mischievously pretty face. Nice-looking boy, Marcel thought.

'My daughter.' Madame Boyer glanced at her watch. 'Isabel.'

The girl's skin was a galaxy of freckles, and she watched him carefully as they shook hands. He sensed something even then, though nothing he could put his finger on. Her breasts were shallow: it took an effort to keep his eyes off them as he asked her age. Fifteen.

'I'm sure Georges won't be long.' Madame Boyer seemed uneasy as she turned her wristwatch on its strap. 'He hardly *ever* goes off like this.'

'Honestly, it's all right,' Marcel said. Isabel shook her hair as she clambered into the pool. Marcel thought of oiled Africans as he added, 'I'm enjoying your remarkable view.'

His business with Boyer went well, and as they finished

talking she whooped past outside, cowboying with the village lads.

'My daughter,' Boyer said.

'Yes.' As he rattled fresh ice, Marcel wondered at the hesitancy of Boyer's pride. 'We met.'

'You thought she was a boy, I suppose?'

'No-o.' A rising inflection in Marcel's tone had questioned the possibility of such an error. Boyer had liked him more.

The train slowed. Vineyards gave way to bungalows and a station name slid past, Coutras. One more stop; then Bordeaux, and home to his wife. He smiled. He and Isabel had got on well from the start; she had even developed a childish crush on him, but six months after their first meeting he had become engaged to Madeleine, whom he later married. As the train began to move again his smile faded. Madeleine was a devout Catholic, and on the morning after their first encounter she had insisted on going to confession. Her face had settled into an expression of piety afterwards and he remembered being entranced by her dark, heavy-lidded beauty as she knelt to say her penance. He wondered how soon he could get her to repeat the sin.

They went to Cap Ferrat that day and Isabel had surprised him, though it was nothing compared to what came later. He had taught her to dive, the roundness of her hips as she paced to the board making him wonder how he had ever mistaken her for a boy, and as they sat on the poolside afterwards Marcel had dozed, the smell of chlorine thick in his head. Madeleine was exchanging cooking hints with Madame Boyer in the kitchen, Boyer growling into a far-away telephone, when her sharp nails raked the thick hair on his shoulder, sending a shiver to his loins.

'You're so hairy, Marcel.' Desire and curiosity were mingled in her voice. '*So* hairy.' She began to rub one small breast against him, its nipple cleaving through his fur. 'Like an ape.' She glanced at the thickening bulge in his trunks. 'A gorilla!'

Marcel had wanted to take her there and then into the pinewoods that surrounded the house, but how could he?

48

The train rushed on and he gazed, sadly now, into the quivering heat-haze outside. Isabel did not go to the church with her parents when he married Madeleine, and afterwards the newly-weds had settled down in Bordeaux. Though the Boyers were a strange couple, Marcel and Madeleine still went often to Cap Ferrat. They had arrived one sunny afternoon to find Madame Boyer poring over bits of junk on her hall-stand. Madeleine had clacked away at once, but Marcel stood politely as the matronly woman prodded a lock-knife, some horseshoe nails, a broken mouth organ, assorted foreign coins. His interest had quickened when he realized she was on the point of tears.

'From Isabel's pocket, Marcel.' There was despair in her voice and she turned to him as though about to confide something momentous, but fear entered her eyes then, and she looked away, saying brokenly, 'She's still a dreadful tomboy, isn't she?'

Isabel, sixteen now, was sunning herself outside. She was wearing tiny briefs. Marcel walked towards her, and, glancing down furtively, he saw tiny golden curls straying from beneath them.

'They say the new Pope will be chosen tonight, Marcel.'

'Oh, yes?'

Later, he sat guiltily beside Madeleine, who had started to read *Le Monde*, and picked up a book. When Isabel stood, he peered over its edge. Her breasts were still flat. Only when she had strolled past did he notice that the page number, 183, was upside down.

The train squealed to a halt. Libourne. He and Madeleine had moved to Lille soon after that: the change had been good for his business, but their marriage was already in trouble. Marcel had been caught out in an affair, and the boy, though willing enough, was embarrassingly under age. The train slid back into motion and he shuddered, remembering their two bleak years in the north. He had found his present house in the pinewoods and was waiting for Madeleine to join him for a final reconciliation when he saw Isabel again. He was passing the high-walled lycée in Saint Hélène one afternoon when she came out of the iron

49

gates ahead of him, carrying books under her arm. Her figure had filled out, but she was the same girl. Marcel smiled when he saw the prongs of a catapult jutting from her jeans pocket, its black sling bobbing as she walked.

'Oh, Marcel!' She turned blindly, butting hard breasts into him. 'Mar*cel*!' They became aware of two of her school-friends, laughing at them from across the street. 'Hold these, mon cher.' Her use of the endearment had shocked him as she cascaded his arms full of books. 'I won't be long!'

She weaved through the traffic and Marcel, embarrassed to see her pointing at him and talking excitedly, looked at the uppermost volume. It fell open at a poem by Malherbe, but it was the margins that held him. They were covered with clear, sensitive observations written in beautiful copper-plate and he thought that the book might once have belonged to Isabel's mother, certainly not to Boyer. He was still engrossed when she reappeared at his side.

'Shameful habit, isn't it?' She grimaced at the exquisitely written notes. 'Didn't you know, Marcel? I'm a terrible egg-head.'

Bordeaux. He left the train and walked into the station car park. He kept his thoughts in the present with an effort as he started up his Citroen, then let himself drift back. She had taken him to a fête at Le Porge the following evening, and when she had tired of dancing she pulled him along a poppied lane into the forest. Her intentions were obvious and excitement had filled him, but fear of her parents finding out, guilt at betraying Madeleine, crowded into his mind.

'Isabel.' He had wanted to stop and talk. 'Listen –'

'Marcel,' she said gaily, 'how can we resist such a force?' She gripped his hand more firmly and pulled him on, adding over her shoulder, 'And why *should* we?'

They kissed for a long time and Marcel, dimly aware that he was about to penetrate her mystery at last, was astonished at her expertise, her hands that were skilled in the ebb and flow of pleasure. It had never occurred to him that she had played *this* game with the airgun-toting boys at Cap Ferrat. Had she? He looked at her face and it seemed

50

unlikely. He undid her jeans button then, and watched her zip whizz down.

'No!' Her hand clutched his. 'Marcel, you *can't.*'

'But, chérie.' He managed a reassuring laugh. 'Is it because' – he hesitated – 'you're a virgin?'

'Yes.' She nodded vigorously, her eyes avoiding his. 'But there's something else, Marcel. Something *more*. You do love me, Marcel? Love *me*, not just' – she grazed his cheek with a filter-tip nipple – 'this?' Silence. When Isabel had read in his eyes a truth Marcel was only just admitting to himself, she lay back with sudden passivity. In a brave, small voice she said, 'Go on, then.'

He slid a hand into her briefs and his fingers touched tiny curls before they froze. Isabel slithered her jeans down shamelessly and exposed her slim, golden body for his pleasure. Her belly was flat and her penis stood up stiffly.

'But . . .' Marcel stared in disbelief. 'Isabel?'

'Now everything will be perfect.' She smiled a freckled smile of happiness and hope. 'Perfect from now on.'

She held his face in her hands and kissed him sweetly. Marcel's senses were still reeling as gladness crept over his shock. His homosexuality had always been a secret thing, a guilty revelling in male flesh that took place at night, in parks and pissoirs. Now, under the open sky with birds singing in the green branches, he explored Isabel eagerly. He shoved her jeans to her ankles, turned her over and touched her bottom. When their panting had subsided, Isabel said, 'Now me, Marcel.' She put her hands in his hair and pushed him down. 'Now me!'

He slowed the car through Saint Hélène, then sped along the forest road for home. The explanation, never asked for, had come in occasional fragments, a still incomplete mosaic in which the obsessive character of Madame Boyer loomed large. She had been convinced from the start of her pregnancy that she would have a daughter, and no one had thought it strange when her baby was delivered at home by an old village midwife. Boyer had not known he had a son until Isabel was six, and she was a girl by then. Marcel smiled as he turned his car

51

around the final curve. Her little grimace as she tucked her balls into her underwear was the most feminine expression he knew.

His wife was waiting on the balcony and their meal was ready. He should have given himself up to the serious business of food then, but as she poured the soup he chuckled, stopping her ladle in mid-air.

'What's so funny, Marcel?'

'Only the usual.' He shrugged. 'Madeleine. Divorce was the Devil's work when I wanted to marry *you*, Isabel, then as soon as she found someone else she sued me for desertion!'

'We got what we wanted, Marcel.' Isabel's wedding ring gleamed as she dunked a savoury biscuit in her Entre Deux Mers. 'Are you complaining?'

'No, no.' He took her hand. 'Only laughing.'

The wine magnified her biscuit until he could see into its pores. When she withdrew it his eyes followed it to her breasts and he felt a sudden, thrilling urge to expose them. Isabel reached for him under the table as he fumbled with her buttons, and they kissed. They were both glad that passion could still strike them so, and they left the soup to go cold. Something hard touched Marcel as he clambered into bed and he lay happily face down, feeling the length of her body as she whispered into his ear.

'Me first, Marcel. Me first!'

LONG TO GO

Joe Mills

'What star sign is Billy? Quick, he's in the bathroom.'

'God! How should I know? One of the fire signs probably – Aries?'

He hung up. Stephen must be desperate, I thought, to start clutching at that sort of straw. Something must have happened.

I tried to put the two out of my mind, but couldn't help imagining poor Billy, eighteen, a daffodil blond, wilting under the heat of Stephen's lust, moving from chair to chair as Stephen became more intoxicated, more daring, more unattractive. Stephen always over-estimated the young's desperation for sex and under-estimated their desire for love. The fact that I had introduced the two made me feel even worse. To Stephen, middle class and middle-aged, anything under twenty-five and aggressively working class was a god. Billy, a sensual-mouthed, donkey-jacketed teenager from the East End of Glasgow was Apollo himself. I didn't know him well, but what I did know was that all the boys round here can smell money a mile off. My asking Billy if he wanted to earn some easy cash was doing them both a favour. If Stephen made a mess of it, he could hardly blame me.

I returned to the bedroom. Andrew's face looked even paler as the cold sunset lined the darkening room with thin bands of yellow. Five years ago, as we attempted to combine our lives, the painting with the writing, the sunsets

53

had been ochre, mustard or even sulphur. I titled Andrew's paintings and re-named the colours on his palette: there were no blues, reds or blacks. They were Ice! Anger! Midnight! He said I was his inspiration.

But those were other rooms in other countries; today the room and the sunset were yellow. For the third time I thought he was dead.

'It was only Susan,' I said hoarsely from the door, afraid to enter the stale-smelling room. 'She was wondering when I would be home: I said next week.'

He was alive.

'Yes. You really must go soon, you know. Your parents will never visit you here – and you can't look after me for ever.'

He was right, of course: the strain was becoming unbearable. But he made me feel guilty by voicing my own anxieties. Sometimes I wished he were dumb, not blind.

I went into the living room and lay down on the sofa, leaving the light turned off. There was an almost prehistoric rhythm to my existence now: the sun would waken me; I would heat the room, go out only if food was wanted, and fall asleep when the sun set. The gradualness of the natural winding down of the day was somehow comforting: dark, darker, sleep – nothing else for it. But this romantic lethargy was becoming addictive: day by day, week by week I found more excuses for doing nothing. If it weren't for Stephen's occasional phone calls I would be doing nothing at all. I had become unable even to summon up the minimal energy required to watch television – besides which I would have felt guilty enjoying the luxuries that Andrew's money provided. Outside was an East End jungle, but inside was a consumer paradise: his art, unlike mine, sold. But I didn't marry him for his money. I didn't.

My being with Andrew simply because of his wealth was, strangely enough, a possibility that seemed to cause him little anxiety; however, there were plenty more insecurities in his mind to prevent him from believing me when I told him that, as far as I was concerned, it was for ever.

'But your twenty-one-year-old for ever is different from my thirty-two-year-old for ever,' he would protest, and we would argue. Despite Andrew's apprehensiveness, he was more secure then about our relationship than not, and we both enjoyed the intellectual arguments. It never occurred to us for a second that 'for ever' would soon become a cruelly redundant phrase.

I had known Andrew three years before he discovered he had the virus. 'Positive,' he said the day he returned from the clinic, the repressed hysteria in his voice underlining the harsh irony of the word.

'Positive,' I said emphatically, optimistically: a command to check the flow of tears and self-pity that would follow if I, too, gave in to despair. At first, cautiously optimistic, my chief emotion was dull, dark confusion – like a parent whose child has disappeared, just after the initial shock has worn off but before time obliterates all hope. When Andrew's condition deteriorated I repressed the confusion and was left simply with a dull numbness. Since he lost his sight I had wandered around the house in darkness; now it seemed unnatural and frightening if a light was switched on by mistake. But, despite the darkness and the quiet, I had no sense of Andrew's following me throughout the house. Whenever I came out of his room, even if I left the door wide open, I felt he stayed there, body and soul. In fact if I glanced at his photo on the wall, or saw his slippers beneath a chair, I would panic with loneliness and rush to his bedside.

I fell asleep on the couch and woke thirty minutes later to the sound of voices outside the house. It was the boys playing football.

'Robert!' Another spasm of guilt: how long had Andrew been shouting? I knew by the grin on his face what it was he wanted. I sat on the hard seat by his bed next to the window, ready for the ritual. 'Describe them to me.'

Andrew was born in the East End of Glasgow; so was I. But we both had a very different recollection of our childhoods. Andrew's earliest memory, he told me, was of loud male voices shouting, challenging and fighting. Whether this was true, or simply the product of a natural desire to romanticise what I knew was a pretty bleak upbringing, was uncertain. We both had different perspectives on our birthplace: unlike me, Andrew had fled the country at a young age. I met him in Spain. I was on holiday; he owned a villa there. I stayed for three years. Andrew's eulogizing of our mutual homeland irritated me. His idealistic memories of 'hard-working, honest, down-to-earth paragons of masculinity' jarred with my own memories of bullies and religious bigots. Nevertheless, he thought it fitting that the sound-track of his earliest years should also be the sound-track of his death. So he had come home to die.

Andrew told me he was happy to lose his sight: his artist's imagination had to work on the sounds he heard, which kept his mind filled when it would have been bored; and the world now, he claimed, was so much better for him because it was almost totally invented by him – and what could be more perfect? Only one thing.

'The only thing better than my imagining is your describing.' Andrew was trying to combine our two worlds again, to make them one, even as he lay on his death-bed. I was to be the artist now, to paint a picture for him, describe the background, the people in the scene, and then (it was a game) to describe details that even I couldn't possibly see.

'It's August,' I said, 'but you can tell it's going to be October in an hour's time. The trees, the grass, the buildings are gold. The sky is crimson – no, yellow: vibrant, like the flame of a match which has just been struck. A grey-black spaceship cloud (October) is on the horizon. Shall I describe the faces in the clouds?'

'No.' He was smiling.

I opened the window. 'The grass has just been cut: smell it. The mower is lying on its side; two winos are sitting on it, drinking, and watching the game. No animals, no parents. Two teams of six.' I opened the window wider. 'I know which team I want to win. All the best-looking boys are in my team: three blonds, and three with dark hair. The oldest-looking dark-haired boy must be nineteen. He's got naturally brown skin, slick greasy black hair – and very hairy legs. He's wearing silver shorts, a shiny blue tee-shirt, and a jumper tied around his waist.'

I didn't mention the bulging crotch, the sweaty nipples, the muscles straining against each other – as I would have done only weeks ago, masturbating Andrew. He couldn't now sustain an erection.

'The tall blond is – oh, he's beautiful, like a sixteen-year-old soldier from the First World War. So fresh-faced and innocent: short blond hair, almost a crew-cut, a dazzling smile, green tee-shirt, white trousers.'

I gazed at this boy for a few minutes. Truthfully he was the only good-looking one there. I suddenly realised that Andrew was crying. Was it because he couldn't see the boy?

'Oh, I can see him all right,' he said. 'He's just like you were when we first met. I can see him in January, the snow melting on his hair, the cold flushing his face red.'

'One of the dark-haired boys has just scored a goal.' There were no cheers; Andrew knew I was lying.

'I remember the day we first met – the way you were so popular with the Spanish boys; and picking up that cat in the street, stroking it – how jealous I was of that cat! How jealous I became of every part of your life that didn't involve me: the time you spent away from me, the people you had known before me: even the characters in your books.'

'You're making me feel very old.' I wiped the tears from his face. But I couldn't bring myself to kiss the chalky skin. It had now been four days since I had last kissed Andrew. I knew that I had now left it too long for me ever to feel comfortable kissing him again. The Last Time We Kissed would be marked in my mind like the memory of a rose dropped carelessly on the ground: it's fallen now; should I stoop to pick it up or go on? There was a trail of them now: the last time I held his hand, the last time we were drunk together, the last time we had sex; each rose became more and more indistinct as time carried us further and further away from it.

'Can I have something to eat?'

We hadn't yet stopped eating together: sharing the cutlery and crockery of a dying AIDS victim was no risk. Even if it had been, I was quite willing to take that risk. The reason? Compensatory Guilt, according to the Books. 'It is very common,' the Books tell us, 'for the healthy partner to attempt to punish himself for his lover's illness due to extreme (and unjustified) feelings of guilt.' This scrap of information was as useless as all the other scraps Andrew and I had garnered from the Books.

Before he went blind Andrew had compulsively devoured every new title – medically informed or simply sensational, every magazine article, TV play or documentary concerning his illness – for some new shred of information. He was as single-minded and thorough in his search as the unattractive man or woman who voraciously reads every new self-improvement manual that appears on the market. That type and Andrew were both looking for the same things of course: a reason, a cure. Andrew, then, had refused to believe he would die of AIDS, just as the unlucky in sex or love sometimes refuse to believe they are incurably unattractive. Would God or Fate be so cruel as to dole out unhappy or foreshortened lives with no apparent rhyme or reason? But Andrew never voiced the bitterness which I knew he must have felt; his anger only revealed itself as a result of some emotional hesitation on my part. He seemed, then, to be reacting less to the idea of his having the disease than to my attitude to it: my refusal to panic or over-react. His behaviour became increasingly unpredictable: one day I was a cold-hearted devil (Didn't I care? Wasn't I secretly pleased? How could I go on as though nothing had happened?) – the next day I was an angel who was suffering in silence to keep him calm.

I wonder now what my feelings for Andrew would have been if he hadn't fallen in love with me so quickly. Would I have loved him more if he had given me another few weeks of uncertainty? I wanted so much to love as he did: with rage and jealousy and single-mindedness. I wanted to think about somebody all the time, to be with him all the time, to relate everything he said or did to our relationship.

A few weeks after our affair began I came across an analysis, in list form, of all my faults and good points. The faults far outweighed the good points – which were themselves ambiguous: ambition, energy. And yet I could find no faults in Andrew to list with such feeling. I enjoyed everything we did together all the time.

58

We ate in the dim light of the street lamp. A cat with slit green eyes peered in through the window, like a judge. The sterile artificial yellow which had replaced the yellow of the sun made all the more noticeable the decrepit state of the room.

'The doctor said that some of the blotches are disappearing,' I said, with all the strained politeness of a relative returning after a two-year absence. Despite Andrew's attempts to maintain our intimacy, we were coming together more and more as strangers in our conversations: but the deception I practised was no mere social politeness; the doctor had said that Andrew's condition was worsening faster than he had thought it would. 'Stephen says there's yet another AIDS play on in London – doing very well too,' I said, immediately regretting it. I was beginning to fall into the trap of well-meaning but unthinking friends who, like the Books, seemed to believe that a fatal illness became more bearable when it was transformed into a multi-media event.

'The blotches aren't disappearing,' Andrew said. 'I can still feel every one of them.' He spoke without emotion, like a character in a detective novel saying "So you see, you must die." 'After all these years you still underestimate my intelligence to' – he began to shake his head – 'oh, to such a degree!'

'The doctor says you're not trying to help yourself.' The truth appeared suddenly in the room of deception, wrenched from me like a demon exorcised by a clever priest who caught it unawares.

'If only I could believe it was because of the illness – but you've always undervalued me – always.' The telephone rang. I let it ring.

'You might still make it,' I said. 'A cure may be found soon.'

'I don't want to make it.'

'Oh, come on! That's just the illness talking!' The demon truth was under control again.

'Do you think if I wanted to survive I would have chosen to stay here rather than go to hospital? Here, with you administering diluted medication, throwing half my drugs out the window?' He glanced angrily towards the ringing telephone.

'I sometimes suspected you knew,' I said, although the possibility had never occurred to me.

'I could have stopped you, but I would have had to leave you. I would be living; you would be living; we would be apart. How could I have stood that?' The telephone finally stopped ringing.

'Don't you have any questions?' I asked him.

'I know there's nobody else. I know you want to be free. I know you'll never be happy.'

'And you know I did it for you.'

'Euthanasia is for those who are left behind. You made a mistake: five years with me. Now you want to wipe that mistake off the face of the earth.'

I took the dirty dishes into the kitchen. Andrew was right all those years ago: his for ever was different from mine. I don't know why it took me so long to realise that. Not a thing in the world could have made me feel more for Andrew, or him less for me. He would never have been able to spend a lifetime (even a foreshortened one) searching for something he had already found. Trying to fall in love again after me, he often said, would have been like trying to learn a language he already knew. It would have been impossible to forget the grammar rules; the vocabulary was already too deeply engrained. The thrill of love, Andrew told me, was the first realisation that it had crept up on you, unnoticed, uninvited.

I want to find that out for myself.

The phone rang again.

'Oh, hi . . . well, I'm sorry that it turned out so badly, Billy. . . He said I would be there too? . . . Wouldn't you have? . . . I wasn't sure. You can never be sure. . . No, I don't care about money, either . . . yes, if you want . . . any day next week.'

It was a start. I put the receiver down, excited, nervous.

I knew now that I hadn't long to go.

JUST ANOTHER SUNDAY

Keith Adamson

Sunday morning, mouth like a cat-tray, duvet half off the bed. No need to get up early, thank God. Len reached out to rummage for his watch which was somewhere among the used handkerchiefs, the ashtray, and the milk-coated glass on the bedside table. Only ten past ten; no hurry. Just another Sunday. He rolled over and pulled the duvet back over his head. There was no sign of Colin. He would be down washing his car. His precious RX 2000.

He didn't stir again until Tara nuzzled the bedroom door open and pushed her cold nose against his bare shoulder, leaving him in no doubt that Colin hadn't fed her. Eleven o'clock. He was feeling muzzy-headed and Tara wasn't going away. Sliding into his slippers he shuffled into the bathroom, where a few drops of water sufficed for the morning's ablutions. Then on to the fridge to locate the half-empty tin of Kennomeat, for the sake of some peace. Colin hadn't bothered to open the lounge curtains; so, still wearing only his slippers, he rectified this, taking a step back as he spotted Mrs McWhirter down in the street on her way home from church. There was no sign of Colin washing the car. No sign of the car.

Over black coffee and burnt toast, he began to re-assemble the jig-saw puzzle of the night before. He had been in the pub with Tom and David when Colin had turned up with Joe and his other cronies from the Theatre Club. They had acknowledged each other when they met at the bar, but Len thought there was little point in introducing Tom and David to all those drama queens, so they agreed to stay in their own groups. Colin remarked that he had designs on the skinny one with the ear-ring. Good luck to him, Len had thought. He was damned if he knew what Colin saw in that creature; but it didn't bother him either way. They had a sort of understanding, Colin and he.

And that's what he'll have done, Len decided. Got off with the actress. Well, so long as he doesn't bring home any camp followers in his knickers again.

There was nothing to do but get the Sunday papers and replenish the milk supplies. Thank God for the Pakistanis! It was only a block away – not worth taking the dog. Sunday morning in this part of town was spot-the-straight time. The place was full of queens. If they weren't out jogging, they were in the Laundromat. And who should be leaving the shop just as he went in there but the skinny one with the ear-ring! For some reason he couldn't understand, Len felt compelled to follow him, at a discreet distance.

The actress turned the corner into Bowmont Street, and disappeared up the second close on the left. Len paused against the railings, lit a cigarette, and tried to look as if he were waiting for somebody. After a minute or two, curtains at a first-floor window were pulled back, and there he was again. Len could picture Colin appearing naked from behind, and draping his arms around this person; but it didn't happen. He waited until he'd finished the cigarette, then, stubbing it out, was about to leave when the actress reappeared at the close entrance, jumped into a car, and was off. Only then did Len realise that the RX wasn't parked in the vicinity.

Back at the flat he decided to give Joe a ring. 'Just wondering if you and Terry wanted to come over some night next week. Supper and drinks. . . ?' They made it Thursday.

'Did Colin get home all right last night?' Joe wanted to know.

Len's heart missed a beat. 'No. Why?'

'Oh, nothing. I just didn't think he was awfully fit to

drive. He was dropping Nigel off . . . and he said he might stop at the park on the way.'

It figured. Nigel lived just round the corner from the park. Well, that was it. There was no way Colin would try anything with Nigel, but if he'd gone to the park he could be anywhere by now.

It had turned into a glorious day – first signs of spring and all that. Len had another cup of coffee and then took Tara down to the riverside walkway, pulling her briskly along. When they came to the bridge she wanted to go the usual route, back along the other side of the river; but Len felt energetic. A runner overtook them, all white poly-cotton and enviable tan, and without warning Tara took off after him, barking and snapping at his heels. Len, em-barrassed, fell into pursuit, calling her back, and shouting that she wouldn't touch anybody. The runner stopped and turned, shoulders heaving, while Tara crouched and growled with convincing menace.

Muttering apologies, Len clipped the lead to her collar. 'She doesn't usually do that'.

'Don't worry.' The runner caught his breath, and flashed a dazzling set of even white teeth. 'Occupational hazard.'

Len found his eyes wandering involuntarily over the well-proportioned body, and caught just a hint that his ap-preciation was reciprocated. Then the runner was off again, a quickly vanishing view of neat bum and sinewy calves. Len stared after him and reflected that Colin would have found a way to establish a link. Somehow he couldn't picture himself managing it.

'Next time,' he said to Tara, 'bite his bum just hard en-ough so we have to take him back to the flat and patch him up.'

She gave him a disapproving look and continued along the path.

The walkway opened into the park, still quiet before the summer rush. Len found himself heading towards the place where the road, a tree-lined avenue, cut across it. There was little traffic, and only one solitary parked car. It was the RX 2000, nose into the kerb, looking abandoned.

He noticed his heart-rate had increased, and there was a rising sense of panic in his throat. Why, for Christ's sake, did Colin feel the need to come to this place in the small hours of the morning? OK, so he'd felt horny. Len had felt the same way half the night, and only the old copies of Zipper under the bed for company. The park was so bloody risky, and he had told Colin often enough.

Tara looked up at him enquiringly – where now? He was damned if he knew. Colin could be anywhere – back at somebody's flat most likely, or shackled to a tree, disfigured out of all recognition.

He crossed the road and headed for the high ground. There was hardly anyone about – just a couple of kids playing at the edge of the river, and an old man picking through the litter bins. Cupping his hands to his mouth, he summoned all his strength and shouted Colin's name, feeling more than a little self-conscious. The two kids looked up, but the old man paid no attention.

'Find Colin, Tara,' he said to the dog. She wagged her tail and licked his face, but didn't understand. One thing was for sure: he couldn't go to the police.

'Come on, Tara.' They went back to the car. Len had the spare keys in his pocket, and considered driving home – but he could hardly do that. Sooner or later, Colin would return expecting to find the car there.

Feeling sick and confused, he let the dog into the back and sank into the driver's seat. He turned on the ignition and pushed home the cassette sticking out of the player – *Bridge Over Troubled Water*. Hah! the irony: it had been their song, at number one in the charts when they first met. He was drumming his fingers nervously on the dashboard when his eye fell on the fuel gauge – it was registering empty.

Hardly had he absorbed the significance of this new evidence, when his thoughts were shattered by an explosion above his head. Hands hammering on the car-roof set Tara jumping against the window and barking furiously. Len whirled round in his seat to find Colin had approached the car unnoticed from behind, accompanied by Nigel. They carried a large petrol can between them; it was obvious Colin had, after all, spent the night at Nigel's flat. Len's relief was like a warm coat on a cold day.

Slowly, he opened the car door. There was no reason to hurry, no urgency to confront Colin. It was, he remembered, just another Sunday.

EMBRACING VERDI

Philip Ridley

I remember the first time I saw Verdi. It was the day we buried Dad and, as our funeral car pulled away from the kerb, I caught a glimpse of him in the rear-view mirror. He was wearing a black leather jacket decorated with studs and splashed with gold. His almost white hair sparkled in the sunlight. Instinctively, I twisted in my seat to stare back at him. As our eyes met, he smiled and waved. Mum tapped my knee and sighed, telling me to sit straight and act properly. It was, after all, a sad occasion and not one for restless fidgeting. But the image of the blond boy haunted me all afternoon. The funeral took second place as my mind created fantasy after fantasy about him. I guessed him to be in his late teens, which seemed ancient to me being only twelve at the time. That night, after the relations had gone and Mum had retired sobbing to bed, I dreamed about him. In this dream I told him all my fears and worries, how I missed my father but was already forgetting him, how I hadn't cried once although I wanted to, and the blond boy embraced me, kissed me and told me his secrets.

Two weeks were to pass before I saw him again. This time he was standing opposite the school gates when I rushed out at four o'clock. The sight of him made me stop dead in my tracks. I felt a strange, tickling sensation in my chest and stomach, like spiders crawling inside. Boys pushed past me, annoyed that I was blocking their way. Since my father's death no one had spoken to me. I think they were afraid of my loss, ashamed of it almost, as if grief

66

and tragedy could be contagious, spread like the common cold.

The blond boy stared at me for a few minutes. Then he strolled across the street. Panic glued me to the pavement. I wanted to run both away and towards him. Finally, he stood in front of me, put his hands on my shoulders and smiled.

'You're Cloud, aren't you?'

I nodded.

'Can I walk home with you, Cloud?'

'Yes,' I said, breathlessly.

Some boys from my class stared at me as I walked down the street with the blond boy. They nudged each other and whispered things, obviously impressed with my new friend. As we walked along, the blond boy hummed an endless succession of haunting melodies. I recognised one or two of them as being from operas. Finally, when we reached the corner of my street, he stopped and murmured, 'This is as far as I can go.'

'Oh,' I said, fumbling for words. Fear of loss, the desire to be with him, made me brave. 'Come home with me. Have something to eat. See my room.'

He flicked sweat from his eyes, squinted against the sun and removed his leather jacket. He wore a white T-shirt, ripped across the chest. I saw his brown skin beneath and one dark nipple. The spiders grew frantic inside.

'Please,' I begged. 'Stay.'

'Perhaps another time.'

'Meet me tomorrow.'

'Don't you want to know who I am?' he asked.

'No,' I said. 'Just meet me.'

'I'm called Verdi,' he whispered. Then walked away.

I watched him until he turned a corner. For a few minutes I just stood there, waiting. For some reason I felt sure he would come back for me. But he didn't. And I went home with an empty feeling where spiders once crawled.

That night, as we ate dinner, Mum started to cry again. She pushed the plates aside and buried her face in the tablecloth. I tried to comfort her, but didn't know the right words. It was guilt more than grief, I think. Dad and Mum had been arguing non-stop for six months before his death. The night he was killed they had been having a particularly violent row. Mum had screamed abuse and accusations. Dad stormed out of the house and drove away in the car: that was the last we ever saw of him. A few hours later, on his way back from wherever he had been, he swerved to miss what he thought was a child and crashed into a letterbox. Ironically, it wasn't a child at all. Just a walking doll set in motion by a couple of pranksters.

I helped Mum upstairs and put her to bed. She took a few of her tranquillizers, asked me to wash up the dinner things and make her a hot drink. Later, as she lay drowsily sipping cocoa, she clutched at my hands and kissed each finger in turn.

'You love me, don't you, Cloud?' she asked.

'Of course.'

'Why didn't *he* love me, Cloud? Tell me that. Why couldn't your father love me? I loved him, you see. I fell in love with him the first time I met him. And I always loved him. No matter what I said, or did, I always loved him. So why couldn't he love me? Am I that difficult to love? Why did he betray me? He was seeing another woman, Cloud. Oh, I know I shouldn't talk ill of him now he's gone, and you'll probably hate me even more than you already do. But you have to know. Otherwise you won't understand what all those arguments were about and why I said the things I said. Oh, he denied it. But I knew! A woman can always tell.'

Every night since my father died I had gone through this ritual with my mother. She would accuse Dad of not loving her, of infidelity, of keeping secrets. I, in turn, would try to convince her that she meant the world to him. Later, she would ask for the photograph album and, laying it across the eiderdown, make me turn the pages as she gave a running commentary on this frozen record of her love for my father. Occasionally she would point to a photograph and say, 'Look. Look at his eyes. He loved me there, you see.' And she would peer intently at the image, squinting hard at the glossy surface, as if trying to see something she had missed before, some clue, some hidden message.

There were photographs of my christening, my first birthday, my first day at school, photographs of me in Dad's arms, kissing him, embracing him, being carried high on his shoulders. Mum would ask me if I remembered it all, and I would answer, 'Yes, yes, everything. I remember it all.' But I didn't. None of the photographs were real for me. None of them reminded me of the vague feelings, growing steadily vaguer, I had had for the man called my father. He didn't look the same in any two photographs. And when I peered at them, bringing them close to my nose, searching as my mother searched for clues and secrets, all I detected was the emptiness behind my father's smile.

That night I dreamed of Verdi again. In this dream we sat cross-legged on a kerb and Verdi showed me a clockwork doll. It had a large brass key protruding from its back and it looked like my father. Slowly, Verdi wound the key and the doll's face clicked into a mechanical smile. Verdi explained there was nothing human inside it, no emotion, no joy, just a complex system of cogs and wheels that gave it a kind of reality. Then he put it on the ground and we watched in wonder as it walked across the street. My mother sat on the opposite kerb. She smiled affectionately when she saw the doll and waited for it with open arms. As its plastic hands touched her knees she squealed with pleasure and embraced it. As one of her hands stroked the doll's hair the other, instinctively, wound the key.

The next morning, at breakfast, I had to suffer her habitual early morning accusations – I no longer remembered my father; I hated him, I was glad he was gone: I was cold, emotionless, self-centred.

'You haven't cried once, Cloud. Not once. If I were to drop dead this very minute, you wouldn't bat an eyelid. Don't you see? It would be so much easier for me if you were to grieve as well. We could comfort each other instead of blocking each other out. You're making me feel like an outcast and I just can't bear it! You make me feel *ashamed* of missing your father! Why are you doing that? Don't you think I had a right to love him?'

I had learnt not to argue with her, not to be drawn into

her world of anger and recrimination. Instead I merely smiled and nodded and ate my cereal. This, of course, was seen as further proof of my heartlessness. She began to poke me in the chest; accusations turned to abuse and insults until I feared for my safety. In desperation, I gathered my scattered books together and rushed from the house.

At school that morning, for the first time since my father's death, boys spoke to me, their curiosity about Verdi overcoming their embarrassment. Where had I met him? Why did he want to be friends with me? Was I about to bleach my hair and spike it up like his? Where did I go with him? Could *they* meet him?

I told them I had been friends with Verdi for ages, went with him to wild dangerous places where all the punks go, that I was accepted by both him and his friends, that I did things my class-mates would never even dream of: I got drunk with Verdi, took drugs, went to frenzied orgies. Verdi was my best friend, the one person I trusted. And I, in turn, was the one person, out of all his many friends, that *he* trusted, the one boy who heard his secrets.

Being seen with Verdi had given me a power and popularity I had never experienced before. Now, through my association with him, boys wanted to be my friend. It was their way – albeit vicariously – of touching him.

That afternoon, at four o'clock, he was waiting for me. I rushed over and grabbed his arm.

'I want you to come somewhere with me,' he said.

'Where?'

'Somewhere special. Somewhere that means a lot to me. A place that meant a lot to someone I used to know. Will you come?'

'Yes. Of course.'

As we walked along, he hummed his operatic tunes and put his arm around my shoulder. I could smell him, the leather and sweat, the lemon-scented aftershave. He walked slowly, his buckled boots jangling with every step like cowboy spurs. He seemed so sharp and clean, glittering like a newly polished diamond. His jeans, bleached almost white, were ripped at the knees and thighs. The body beneath was hard, unyielding, like peeled wood.

I followed him blindly, content just to be with him. We walked down some stone steps and then along the banks of the canal. After a while Verdi stopped by a large grey stone and sat on it. He took off his leather jacket, lay it on the grass and told me to sit down.

'It's nice here,' he said. 'It's a good place to come and think.' He gave me one of his usual sad smiles. 'Do you like it here, Cloud?'

'Oh, yes.'

'Good.'

I lay my head against his knees. He hummed his melodies and stroked my hair. The touch of his fingers made the now familiar spiders scamper in my stomach.

'What tune is that?'

'It's opera,' he answered. 'I love opera, you see. It's all I can listen to. The only thing that means anything. That's how I got my nickname. Someone said I should be called Verdi because I was always humming opera. So that's my name now. Just think: I had to wait eighteen years to know my real name!'

'My name's a nickname too,' I said. 'My father gave it to me. He always said I went round with my head in the clouds, so he called me Cloud.'

'He knew a lot then, your father.' Verdi cupped my head in his hands and stared into my eyes. 'What was he like? Tell me about him.'

'Who?'

'Your father.'

'Oh, he's dead.'

'But tell me about him, Cloud. Just because he's dead doesn't mean there's nothing more to say. Was he cheerful? What did he do at home? Tell me things, Cloud. You're his son. You must know things. Did you love him?'

The question took me by surprise. I pulled away from Verdi and stood up. He frowned. I tried to think of something to say, something that would please him and make him desire me. There was a desperate, pleading look in his eyes: so I told him what he wanted to hear.

'Oh, yes,' I said. 'I loved him. I loved him more than anything. He was my whole world to me. Sometimes I dream that he's still alive. But when I wake up I realise that he's gone, and I cry. I miss him more and more. He did things for me, you see. Told me stories. Yes. I remember now. He told me stories before I went to sleep.' I hadn't thought about this before, but now, carried away by my fluent improvisation, the memory came back, vivid and real and I stood there, amazed that I had forgotten something that had once meant so much to me. 'Yes,' I continued, sitting beside Verdi again, clutching his legs, resting my chin on his knees. 'He told me lots of wonderful stories. No one tells me stories any more.' And suddenly I was crying. All the grief I had buried with my father rose inside me, a bitter distress that left me numb.

Verdi kneeled beside me and cradled me in his arms. I felt his breath, hot against my neck. As we embraced each other, our lips met and he kissed me. It was a gentle, comforting kiss that quelled the spiders.

Afterwards, he untucked his tee-shirt and dried my eyes. As he pulled me to him, I reached out and lay my hands against his bare stomach. I felt as if my blood flowed through my palms and into his body.

'Cloud,' he whispered. 'Will you do something for me? Even though it seems strange? Will you do something for me without asking why?'

'Of course,' I said. 'Anything.'

'I want a photograph of your father. Make it the most recent you can find. Will you do that for me?'

'Yes,' I said.

Verdi stood up and said he had to go, but he would meet me the next day. When I asked where, he replied, 'Here. The secret place.'

After he had gone I sat alone for a while, watching the sunlight sparkle across the surface of the canal and listening to the water trickle. I was filled with a joy I had never experienced before, a warm contentment that made me calm.

That night, as Mum sipped cocoa in bed, I got the photograph album without waiting to be asked, and lay it across her lap. Immediately, I turned to the back of the book where the most recent pictures were. She watched in wonder as I examined each in turn.

'Oh, Cloud,' she sighed. 'You do miss him.'

There was only one photo of both me and my Dad. It was important Verdi have an image of me as well. I took it from the album.

'Can I have this?' I asked. 'To keep?'

'Oh, yes,' she said, hugging me, kissing me. 'Of course, Cloud. See how much he loved you! You can see it in his eyes and smile.'

'Yes,' I said. 'I see.'

That afternoon, as planned, I returned to the secret place by the canal. Verdi was waiting for me. He asked me to sit beside him. Putting his arms round my shoulders he kissed the top of my head and asked, 'Did you bring it?'

'Oh, yes,' I said, handing him the photograph. 'It was taken at Easter. Just a month or so before he died. That's me before I had my hair cut. Do you recognize me?'

Verdi nodded. He stared in silence at the photograph: his hands were trembling. I asked him what was wrong. He shook his head and held me tighter, clutching me so hard it hurt, squeezing the air from my lungs. It was as if he wanted to crush me into his body, make me part of him.

'Verdi!' I gasped. 'Let me go!'

He was crying – a helpless, desperate sobbing that shook his whole body. Finally, with a yell so loud birds exploded from nearby trees, he fell to the grass. The photo was screwed to a ball in his hands.

'Verdi,' I said. 'Please don't cry, Verdi.'

Gradually, the tears stopped, but it was a slow process, and by the time he had regained composure, the sun was setting and the sky was streaked with red. He picked grass from his mouth and smiled.

'I'm so popular now,' I said. 'All the boys in my class want to be my friend. It's because of you, Verdi; because of you.'

He kissed my cheek, smoothed the photograph against his chest, then slipped it into his jacket pocket and stood up. He looked down at me and touched my hair.

'Will you meet me tomorrow?' I asked.

'Perhaps not.'

'Oh, no, Verdi!' I stood up and grabbed him round the waist. 'Verdi, you mustn't go!'

He held me at arm's length and stared into my eyes.

'Just because you can't see me doesn't mean I'm not around, Cloud,' he said. 'You're popular now. People like you. That's a rare gift. I'm going now. Don't follow me. Thank you for the photograph.'

I watched him walk away. He didn't look back once. I sat alone by the canal for over an hour.

When I got home I went straight to my room and fell on the bed. Before long Mum came up. She sat on the edge of the mattress and ran her hand up and down my spine.

'Come on,' she said. 'No one is ever gone. He's still with us. You were lucky to know him. Just don't forget what he's taught you and he'll always be with you. Nothing is for nothing.'

I hadn't heard her sound so joyous and confident. I sat up and looked at her. Her face was brave.

'Come on,' she said again. 'It's time we sorted through his clothes. Help me. It's time to move on.'

We went to her room and opened Dad's wardrobe. One by one she laid his suits and jackets on the bed. Carefully, we went through the pockets; bus tickets, half-eaten sweets, bits of fluff. She made a pile for jumble and a pile of things she thought would be useful for me one day.

There was one jacket left in the wardrobe. I went to get it and sat on the bed, laying it across my lap. In the breast pocket I found a photograph. I looked at it and my heart froze.

'What's that?' Mum asked, putting the jumble into an old suitcase.

'Oh, nothing,' I said, slipping it into my pocket. 'Nothing at all.'

Mum came over and kissed me.

'I love you, Cloud,' she said. 'Really.'

'Yes,' I said. 'I love you.'

That night, as I lay in bed, I looked at the photograph of Verdi I had found in my father's jacket pocket. I tried to take in every detail of the image; Verdi sitting on the rock at the secret place, his jacket slung casually over his shoulder,

74

his blond hair glittering in the sunlight. But there was something different about him. Something that, at first, eluded me. Then I realised what it was: he was happy. His smile was so wide and so joyous it made the spiders crawl in my stomach. And I had never seen him happy before. It transformed his whole face, made him younger, brighter, more real. But there was a shadow at the bottom of the picture: my father, as he stood with the sun behind him, taking the photograph. I stared at the shadow.

DOMINOES, DRAUGHTS AND TEA

Ian Hutson

'I don't care what it costs – within reason. – This is our first anniversary; it's your birthday next week and mine the month after. We're going, and the money is coming out of the Building Society to do it. Sod rainy days! They don't cost more than any other.'

'You're determined?'

'I am.'

'Well in that case you won't mind me selling part of my stamp collection to finance California in July.'

'But. . .'

'No buts. If you can blow it so can I and that is that.'

The final three words were spaced out and given emphasis to a degree which finished the discussion.

'Moreover, I intend enjoying it to the full and I suggest you do the same. If you wish to feel guilty, please do so whilst at home.'

'A fine picture of a clown you'd make, celebrating someone else's birthday and an anniversary in Vienna on your own! I guarantee it won't be *me* who's the first to suggest a "quiet" day to rest an aching back and sore feet. . . We'll confirm the booking tomorrow.'

The two fell quiet for a while, concentrating on eating, because the main course had arrived somewhere between California and Vienna. Mr Avison had decided on sole whilst Mr Stimson was tucking into his usual steak. Mr Avison looked across with a wry grin as he poured another glass of rosé – his compromise between the proprieties of white with fish and 'something red and very heavy' (as Mr Stimson always said) with steak.

'Nor will I be the one to demand the attentions of the hotel's doctor and "simply insist" on an "essential" daily massage to cure the back-ache brought on by a quick jog up a flight of fancy.'

'That, as you well know, is grossly unfair and uncalled-for! It was no flight of fancy but all the steps in the Tiger Balm Gardens. If you had carried your fair share of suit-cases on the first day I would not have missed half the New Year celebrations. I was in pain – can I help it if the only available doctor is Chinese, about twenty-five and extremely good-looking? How could I argue if he prescribed regular massage? Be fair! Pass the mustard.'

'I seem to recall that the onset of this "damn near slipped disc" occurred very soon after you caught sight of the masseur by the staff entrance.'

'Hong Kong was your idea, not mine.'

'But you enjoyed it.'

'Of course! But I am simply saying that if you intend getting insanely jealous of every spring chicken who walks past perhaps we ought to cancel Vienna and find a monastery somewhere.'

Mr Stimson chased a roast potato around his plate. 'That would be putting the cat amongst pigeons! You well know what you're like with uniforms. . .'

'Habits.'

'Bad ones, and quite uncontrolled.' Mr Stimson snorted and stabbed another roast potato with unnecessary energy.

'I was thinking we could go to Brighton again first – drive down on the Wednesday perhaps and stay at the "King Edward"? It's nice this time of year, not so crushed as in the silly season.'

'Fine. It'll split up the travelling – less of a drive before flying.'

They continued to eat for a while in silence, ignoring the hubbub of noise in the restaurant and oblivious to much, except what was on their plates. Each mouthful was savoured and relished, appreciated for its full worth. The plates hardly needed washing up once they'd finished. Mr Stimson chuckled over his glass and the laughter lines around his eyes crinkled. 'Nothing really. I was just remembering you in that floating restaurant. Insisting on "going ethnic" and having chopsticks.'

'So?'

'Don't you remember? You'd ordered steak as usual and by the time you realised you had no knife and fork the waiter had taken the hump and disappeared.'

'Hm. Trust you to get a picture of me chomping at an extremely rare lump of bull using my fingers. No sane person going to a restaurant at night carries a camera. How come you just happened to have one, complete with flash unit?'

'Years of disciplined planning and a bad memory. I'd forgotten I was carrying it until it came in useful. As I remember it you were also drunk at the time.'

'Since I'm usually only about two drinks behind you I can believe it. Whistle at the waiter.'

'Pardon?'

'Sweet.'

'Yes, I realise he is, but. . .'

'Don't be obtuse. I want a sweet tonight, so kindly use your charm to attract the waiter. Hot fudge cake with cream. Possibly twice. I'm not sure yet.'

'Pig.'

'Thank you. That's the nicest thing you've said to me all day.'

'Not true! Why, I complimented you on your sartorial taste only seconds before we left home.'

Mr Avison stared heavenwards. 'I hardly think "Gor blimey guv, where did you get that 'at" constitutes a compliment.'

'It had the desired effect – you left the hat behind.'

'I happen to be fond of that hat.'

'I can imagine! It must have been in the family for years. Cheeseboard?'

'In due course, Mr Stimson. In due course.'

They doodled with the remaining cutlery until the coffee arrived, glancing at each other over the flickering candles.

'Incidentally, Mr Stimson, how much is Vienna going to cost?'

'Money and fair words – my treat. Providing you pay tonight.'

'Any idea of what we have left in the collective kitty? I hope you've been keeping track because I haven't a clue.'

Mr Stimson reached into his left jacket pocket for his calculator and produced it with a flourish. He played with the keys for a few moments, although he knew to the penny what their assets were. 'Including your sister's bits and bobs?'

'Yes.'

'With or without the speeding fines?'

'With. All except last Tuesday's. I have no intention of paying that one – the policeman was rude.'

'At the present rate of expenditure we'll both be destitute in three years and four months. Relatively destitute – but on target at least.'

'In three years and four months we'll both be too far gone to make it to the post office. Throw away the calculator and think of somewhere else to go – August is free, isn't it?'

The waiter brought more coffee without being asked – an advantage of their being regular customers (and old-fashioned tippers).

'How long have I known you?'

Mr Stimson reached again for his calculator. 'Exactly?'

'No, roughly will do, thank you.'

'Eighteen months and two weeks on Thursday.'

'And we've lived together for a year.'

'That is the general idea of an anniversary.'

'Before I met you I could have lived without ever having to touch my pension at all. Do you realise I'll be broke now in three years?'

'And four months.'

'I was allowing for inflation.'

'So was I.'

'Do you know what?'

'What?'

'I wish I'd met you fifty years ago.'

They both went quiet.

'You're a silly old seventy-two-year-old and you know we wouldn't have got on at all well then.'

'Don't spoil it. I like to think we would have been the same. Certainly if we had met earlier we wouldn't have ended up playing draughts at a Community Centre, catching each other out making spaniel looks at passers-by.'

'We would have worn ourselves – and probably half the world – out. May do yet.'

'But you are glad we met?'

There was a pause.

'I've never been happier. As you say, my only – small – regret is that I had to wait until now to have the time, wherewithal and sense really to enjoy life a little. I don't even mind the sense of urgency now because, I suppose, I've really always felt that. We're going out of the world broke and laughing our socks off – and not too far apart. Still agreed?'

'Agreed.'

They finished their coffee and waited for the brandy to arrive.

'I'll regret this in the morning.'

'No-one's forcing you to eat.'

'True. I have always wanted to write a thesis on extended indigestion around the world.'

'Mr Stimson?'

'Yes.'

'Walk me home.'

Both left tips under the edge of their plate for the waiter with the tight black Farrahs and the puppy-dog smile.

'How many first editions do you have left exactly?'

'I forget, Mr Stimson. Ask the insurance company. Why?'

'Well, you remember that documentary on the U.S.S.R.?'

'Oh. Red Square in August? Why not; it always reminds

me of the Bond films, and when we're both dead what use will the Exchequer have for a leather-bound set of whatever they were?'

'Just don't wear that idiot hat – we don't want any international incidents. They might take our passports away.'

NOTHING LIKE

Rodney Mills

Geoff Grant was surprised when Keith Fletcher came up to him in the staff room before school began. They didn't usually have much to say to each other. They had different ideas about discipline: Keith was a hard-liner – give them a good kick and keep them in their place. He didn't approve of the methods Geoff used as a Year Head – all talk and sympathy, and saying they were good boys. The pupils called Keith Rat-Face, and with his small bristly moustache, pinched cheeks and sharp protruding fangs, it wasn't difficult to see why.

'Can I have a word?' Keith asked. He looked suspiciously round the crowded room, and it was clear that he wanted a word in private. Geoff became apprehensive. One of his boys was probably in trouble, had done something or said something that Keith considered disgraceful and needed to be dealt with. 'Disgraceful' was one of Keith's favourite words.

'OK,' said Geoff. They went into the corridor. 'What is it?'

Keith waited until the secretary had gone by and disappeared into the staff room before he said, 'It's Barry Walsh.'

Geoff groaned inwardly. Barry was one of his fifth-formers who always had too much to say for himself and was for ever getting teachers' backs up.

'I was taking detention last night,' Keith went on, 'and Walsh was there – as usual. It was near the end. They'd finished the work that had been set, and they began to talk and ask questions. You know the way they do. About sex and things, trying to get you embarrassed. I didn't mind; I can manage them. It was just a way of filling in the last few minutes, so it was all right. And then Walsh just came out with it. I was very angry, I can tell you.'

Keith's face was angry now as he remembered.

'Came out with what?' Geoff asked.

'He said, "Mr Grant's a pouf".'

Geoff tried to prevent himself from betraying any emotion, but his face suddenly flushed, and he could feel his skin burning.

Keith hurried on. 'Someone was talking about dirty old men in the park, and Walsh just came out with it.'

'What did you do?' Geoff asked, trying to sound calm.

'I told him not to be impertinent. It was disgraceful, talking about a teacher like that. I said I'd report him to you. You're his Year Head.'

School was about to begin, and activity in the corridor had increased with teachers hurrying to their classrooms. Geoff didn't want the whole school to know, though no doubt they soon would. Keith enjoyed relaying to the rest of the staff at great length incidents of delinquent behaviour that proved liberal methods didn't work.

'I thought you ought to know,' said Keith. He sounded disappointed that Geoff's response hadn't been more violent.

In fact, Geoff had been so stunned that he hadn't known how to react. How would someone be expected to behave on hearing news like that? Become angry? Express horror and revulsion? He decided it was better to go on playing it as coolly as he could.

'Thanks,' he said. 'I'll see to it.'

'It's disgraceful,' said Keith, working himself up into a passion. 'Walsh ought to be beaten for saying a thing like that.'

Geoff's face closed up with disapproval. He didn't believe in using brutal methods against children.

'OK. Leave it with me. I'll think about it.'

He thought about it for the rest of the day.

He supposed he was grateful to Keith for telling him. It was just as well to know what was being said behind your back. But he was angry too. How could Keith have let a situation like that develop? It was one thing for boys to snigger among themselves and speculate about the private lives of their teachers. Something else altogether to blurt it out loud to a member of staff! Keith shouldn't have let it happen. Funny how it was always the hard disciplinarians that pupils were rude to or tried to shock.

Well, it was done now. The problem was how to deal with it. He felt he would *have* to take some action; he couldn't let boys go around saying things like that about him. It could finish his professional career. He could get the sack.

Numb with worry, he somehow registered his class, dealt with three of his fifth-year pupils who had problems, and taught a double period of English to a third-year class. Then it was break, and he was on playground duty. With a mug of coffee in his hand, he picked his way through some small boys scurrying across the asphalt in pursuit of a tennis ball. The fifth-year boys – his boys – usually congregated round the door of the toilets, gossiping, winding each other up, on the look-out for a quick smoke. Geoff glanced across at them. Barry Walsh was there in the middle of a gang of his mates.

He was a big boy, well-developed for a sixteen-year-old. Geoff had watched him doing weight training and had been impressed by the solid arms and thighs, the muscles, the polished black skin. He was often in trouble for talking out of place or being aggressive. But he had an engaging sense of humour and was usually high-spirited and extrovert. Geoff liked him. He thought he had a good relationship with him. The boy always had a smile and a cheery greeting for him when they passed in the corridor.

So what had made him say it? Was he just being malicious? Or did he suspect something?

Geoff had always been very careful. He was sure his manner gave nothing away. He had never made approaches to a pupil. Not that he was entirely immune: some of the boys were very attractive. When he sat down beside a boy to correct his work, the boy's thigh would sometimes press against his under the desk. But he never took advantage of the situation.

So how had this happened? He dragged his eyes away from Barry and his friends and strolled to the other end of the playground. What was he to do about it? Summon Barry and have it out with him? Demand what he meant by it? Tear him off a strip for being offensive? Because he would have to take some action. He couldn't just let it go.

But by the end of the day, he had still done nothing.

Paul was late home. Geoff remembered he had said something that morning about a meeting after school. He watched from the window for a sign of Paul's car, then he paced impatiently up and down the room, desperate to talk to somebody.

When he heard the key in the latch, he hurried out to greet him.

'I'm glad you're back,' he said. 'Something dreadful's happened.'

Paul dumped down a pile of books. 'God, what now?' He looked tired and despondent. He had his own worries.

'How did the meeting go?' Geoff asked.

'Oh, the usual thing,' Paul said. 'Anyone who doesn't wear school uniform should be hanged, drawn and quartered. Now what's your problem?'

'It'll keep,' said Geoff. 'I'll tell you over dinner.' He went into the kitchen to begin preparing the meal. 'Don't worry.'

It was not until they were sitting down over coffee that he told Paul what had happened.

'It's nothing,' Paul said. 'You're well aware what kids are like. They think they're so sophisticated and know everything. But at sixteen, they still don't know they've even been born. He was just trying it on. It doesn't mean a thing.'

Geoff was not so sure. 'Keith Fletcher thought it was serious enough to come and tell me about it.'

'From what you've said about Keith Fletcher, he'd latch onto anything that could get a kid into trouble.'

'What do you suggest I do about it then?'

Paul suddenly swung round to stare at Geoff. 'You're not thinking of doing a big Gay Pride thing, are you? Coming out?'

The idea had passed through Geoff's mind. He thought it might simplify things. It was so difficult – and so dangerous – living the kind of lie he was living. He said as much.

'You must be crazy,' Paul retorted. 'You know what the kids think about gays! They just haven't enough experience of life to understand. They've been brainwashed by what they've seen on TV or read in the *News of the World*. You wouldn't stand a chance; all the good you do for those kids would just go down the tube. They wouldn't trust you again, or come to you for help.'

'You think so?'

'I know so.'

'Then what?'

'Ignore it. Forget about it. If you make a fuss, it'll just make it worse. The lady doth protest too much, and all that. Don't do anything, leave it alone. It'll soon die down. You know what kids are like! They say all sorts of things about their teachers, so why should anyone believe them or think twice about it?'

Geoff brooded over what Paul had said, but he was not convinced.

'Come on,' said Paul. 'Let's watch that tape we made of *The Alternative Miss World*. It'll cheer you up.'

It didn't. Paul hooted at the antics of the transvestite competitors, but Geoff couldn't share his delight. That was probably how Barry and his friends thought of him – someone with a man's body who behaved like a woman.

When they went to bed, Paul wanted to make love. He put his arm round Geoff's waist, began to kiss his neck and press against him. Geoff grunted and lifted Paul's hand away. He shifted along the bed and dug deeper into the pillow. He had too much on his mind.

As Geoff finished taking the register next morning, Barry Walsh came into the classroom. For one awful moment, he thought the boy had come to denounce him to his face, and his heart gave an uncomfortable lurch. But a quick glance at Barry suggested that this was unlikely: he was looking miserable and depressed, quite different from his usual exuberant self.

'Can I see you, sir?' he asked.

'Of course,' Geoff said. 'What's up?'

Barry eyed the boys still dawdling over getting their books together for the day and arguing about last night's TV. 'Can I see you alone?'

'If you like,' said Geoff. 'We can go to the interview room.'

He was free next period so he would have the time.

On their way there, Geoff wondered if he had been sensible in agreeing to see Barry alone. Heaven knew what the boy might say to Keith Fletcher next time he was on detention. But Geoff was Barry's Year Head, and he had his job to do. The boy obviously needed help of some kind, and he couldn't allow anything to interfere with that. He had decided to take Paul's advice – carry on as though nothing had happened. They went inside and sat down on the easy chairs, facing each other.

'Now, what is it?' Geoff asked.

Barry darted a quick look at his teacher and then lowered his head. His heavy lower lip hung open and his pink tongue licked nervously at it. He looked so embarrassed that for a moment Geoff wondered if he had come to apologise, but then Barry pressed his lips together resolutely and began.

'I got picked up by the police last night,' he said. He explored Geoff's face for a reaction before going on. 'It was in the shopping centre. I was waiting for a bus home when these two policemen came up to me and accused me of pinching someone's handbag.'

'And had you?' Geoff asked.

'No!' Barry exploded. 'I was just standing there, waiting for my bus.'

'All right, Barry,' Geoff said, soothingly. 'Keep calm. I believe you. Then what happened?'

'They took me down to the station. They've charged me.'

'Do your parents know?'

'Yes. My Mum had to come to the station to collect me. She said to see you. Ask you what to do.'

It was an all-too-common problem. Geoff had had to deal with many cases like this. There was not much the school could do except be sympathetic and give its support.

'How did the police treat you?' Geoff asked.

Barry knew what the teacher meant. 'They were all right,' he said.

'You'll need a solicitor. I'll phone Mr Brown at the Race Relations Centre. He'll be able to help.'

Geoff went to the desk and picked up the phone. While waiting for a line, he studied Barry. The boy was slumped back in his chair, deflated and defeated, his legs spread open in front of him. His weight training had certainly developed his thighs.

What was the boy's sexual experience? Geoff was sure that all the girls would fancy him, and he had the kind of physical arrogance that implied he had had many successes and could easily choose. Yet Geoff knew that all this talk of teenage promiscuity was absurdly exaggerated. Barry was probably still a virgin. Perhaps even anxious and uncertain about his own sexuality. Was that why he had said what he had said? Testing and trying it out? Well, Geoff had no intention of helping him discover what he was.

Mr Brown came on the line, and Geoff explained the situation. Barry watched him with wide, solemn eyes.

'What's he like? Well . . . he's lively.' He pulled a face at Barry, and the boy grinned briefly before becoming serious again. 'But I can't believe he'd do something like this. I'd be quite happy to go to court as a character witness. . . You can see him this afternoon at four o'clock?' Barry nodded his agreement. 'Right. He'll be there. Thanks a lot.' Geoff put the phone down.

He moved to the front of the desk, and Barry got to his feet.

'Mr Brown will look after you all right,' Geoff said. 'He'll arrange for a solicitor. So there's no need to worry.'

He was about to pat the boy on the back to reassure him and then thought better of it. They were standing very close together. They were the same height.

Barry seemed to become bashful. He lowered his eyes and then flicked them up quickly. 'Thanks, sir,' he said. Geoff noticed how long his black eyelashes were.

'That's OK. Let me know what happens.' He opened the door so that Barry could leave.

The boy took a couple of steps and then turned. He was still hanging his head as though embarrassed or ashamed. His tongue darted out to lick his lips.

'I suppose Mr Fletcher told you,' he said.

Geoff was immediately on his guard. 'Oh that. Yes.'

'I'm sorry. I shouldn't have done it.'

'Don't worry about it.'

Barry raised his head as though he had got rid of a great burden. He smiled and gave a chuckle. 'I don't know why I said it. You're nothing like a pouf!'

For a moment, Geoff thought he was going to strike out and knock that silly grin off the boy's face. He could feel a surge of anger sweep through him. But then, with a great effort, he checked himself. He forced himself to grow cool and still. He even managed a modest smile.

'That's all right, then,' he heard himself say.

Still grinning, Barry nodded and went out of the office. Geoff stared blankly after him.

ROOM WITH NO VIEW

Martin Foreman

I hate this room. I hate the fact that it is always dark, that on days when the sun actually lies for an hour or so at the bottom of the bed I must close the curtain against the curiosity of passers-by. I hate the dirt that lies thick where it cannot be seen, the grease stains that I cannot remove, the peeling and grubby paint. I hate this room because it *is* my room, because it is all I have, because no matter how far into the future I look I can seen nothing but these four walls, this ceiling, that door. I hate this room because it is nothing, has nothing, not even a prospect, not even a view.

He lies here asleep, breathing so lightly that the cover does not move. His head and shoulders and an arm sprawl across the pillow, showing me the spots that lie thick on his back. When I first saw him I looked with more curiosity than desire, impressed only by the thick black hair that swept up and tapered like an arrow. He caught my stare and for some reason grinned; without thinking, a reflex from the past, from countless nights in bars and discos, I winked and saw him wink at me.

When we came in, I wanted to rush into the bathroom, to shower away two days of dirt and endless weeks of loneliness, but he held me and kissed me and sniffed me as urgently as if he were seeking something of great value. I tried to respond, but I could only watch his pale, elongated body as it emerged from its clothes, his hands as they undid and pulled off my trousers and shirt, his expression as he pushed and pummelled me this way and that, as he moved frantically over me, as his mouth hung open in a deepening silent cry, as his hips and body jerked. I stared, amazed, for I could not remember anyone coming like that, anyone so lost. I envied whatever took him out of himself, his world, this room.

Now the pall of sex lies thick and warm. If I could somehow touch it, hold it, concentrate it, inhale it, I would understand what moved him, what possessed him, this strange secret he has. Did I ever make love like that? Did I ever lose myself so completely? I cannot remember. I cannot even remember those I have made love to; I see only disconnected faces, bodies, buttocks, groins.

He sits opposite me at the other end of the bed drinking tea. We have made love again, slowly, intensely, our bodies coming together like a strong tide, each individual movement a scarcely noticed ripple of waves. This time I was swept up; I had to take part. He hypnotised me with the staring eye that came together in the middle of his face as we kissed, his tongue pressing deeper and deeper into my mouth, pushing me back onto the bed and forcing me to close my eyes and give myself to him. And as the orgasm, the tide, came near, I did not know whether it came from within me or without; I felt myself explode and when it was over I had to hold him and hold him and hold him until my body had become mine again and I was no longer afraid.

His name is Eric. He once worked in a bakery; he usually signs on the day before I do. He lives not far from here, with his parents, no longer tries to look for work, spends his days listening to music, wandering the streets, combing his hair. His voice is quiet and heavy with accent, suggests strength and anger and pride. He frowns, doesn't like being questioned, asks no questions in return. Curiosity, I realise, is no more than habit, an impulse which destroys as much as it explains. The more I ask about the outside world, the more I remind him of it and encourage him to return. So I stop, say nothing, watch and wait.

He tells me he is hungry and asks if I have food. The

91

cupboard is beside him; there is, as always, pasta and baked beans, and I can find an old tomato and cheese. He stands watching as I cook and without turning my eye I see the arch of his nose, the roughness of his chin and cheek, the thin, hard body that waits, that calls out to me from under his shirt; and I think of his prick, long, curved and almost deformed, the hair that curls, as if surprised by itself, over his buttocks and legs. But that is only part of him; it bothers me that I cannot remember whether his body was warm or cold, that I have forgotten his smell, which now lies buried under the steam of macaroni and sauce.

He squats on the bed, plate in hand, as I fiddle with the aerial. I join him and we watch the cartoon; I am surprised that the day has gone; it is late afternoon. He watches intently, laughing at the absurdities on the screen, only occasionally looking down to guide food onto his fork. Because he laughs, I laugh with him, and these talking cats, these black and grey figures, are not only comic but erotic, pervaded with his presence, his body, his lust. I reach out a hand and place it on his knee. He ignores it. I move it onto his thigh. I sense his tension and quickening of breath.

We have watched everything, game shows and comedies, soap operas and the news. We have moved our bodies again and again, searched for the ideal position of comfort with each other and the bed. Now he is stretched out, head propped up by the pillow and his hands. I kneel over him, staring at each fold of his shirt, at the stains and tears in his trousers. I touch him, hold him, stroke him. I release the button and zip and pull his trousers down to his thighs, push up the shirt and reveal his prick; the suggestion of muscle, the abstract pattern of hair, the shadow that glides down to bury itself between his legs, are all so beautiful, so breath-taking, that I am almost afraid to go on.

He is in the bathroom, preparing for the night. I don't want anyone to see him, to remind him that there are others but me. As I was making love and he lay hardly responding, I thought I heard him cry. 'Do you want me to stop?' I asked. 'No,' he said, 'no, no!' almost desperately, like a plea. When I came, collapsed and rolled off him, he pulled my face to his and kissed me with a harsher urgency than when we came in. 'I love you,' he whispered and I wondered if I'd heard.

We lie squashed together in the dark and he asks the kind of questions I asked him before. I tell him about my family, that I don't see them any more. 'Why?' Because they live two hundred miles away, because we've never been close, because they're part of a past which is long dead and gone. I tell him about university and the fact that I've only ever had summer jobs. 'What kind of work d'you want?' The question is strange: I don't know. Months, years ago, I used to write to companies, to libraries, to newspapers, to advertising agencies, but they all turned me down. I no longer think about work, hardly know what it means.

He asks about those I've slept with before. In the days when I had money I would go out every night to pick someone up, but I've never lived with anyone, never seen the same person more than a few times. He finds that odd, and tells me about the girl he went out with for over a year and the boy who lived in the same block, who played football every week. Then he stops, unwilling to talk any more, rests his head between my shoulder and the pillow and soon, very soon, is asleep.

I do not know how long I have been staring up at the ceiling. There is little to see but thick shadow; all the stains and marks I look at in daytime have gone. I am not comfortable – he has pushed me into the corner, yet still grasps my waist – but that is not the reason why I cannot sleep. The room has changed – its walls and curtain are the same; its heavy furniture still presses into the middle; the carpet, so old that its pattern has faded, is no less ugly. I used to feel oppressed, weighed down, but that feeling has gone. I feel somehow lighter, a little less real.

I can just make out in the darkness his hair crushed and tangled on the pillow, a suggestion of beard on his cheek, his mouth half-open as he breathes. Now I notice his smell. His body stretches beneath the covers and each position he shifts into is more attractive, more sexual than the last.

My emotions are frozen; I dare not think or remind myself I am alone. He promised to come back. I don't know if he will. Only to go home, to change his clothes, he said, both pleading and defiance in his voice. I watched him through the window, and felt I had died when I could no longer see him.

I should tidy up, put some order in this room, make it attractive. I look around me and wonder where to begin. Bed, wardrobe, cooker, chair all stare back at me, challenging me to move them, clean them, create a better home. There is no point. With one of my last coins I go and shower, wash away the dirt, the smell, and the past.

I did not realise how handsome he could be. His face has resolved into angles of personality; he has shaved and re-done his hair and put on bright clothes. 'Take this,' he says, handing me a carrier bag, then puts his arms around me and we kiss. My tongue probes, my hands begin to feel under his belt, but he draws away and asks, 'Well, aren't you going to have a look?' I open and pull out packets and cans and vegetables. At first I do not understand; then he tells me that he borrowed money from his sister, that it is a present, that it means we do not have to go out. An image of the street, of shops and queues, of people talking and moving and jostling, returns like the memory of an unpleasant dream.

We have soup, sausages, potatoes and eggs. As we eat, I look up from the bed to see someone peering in. A woman's face, turning away as she walks by, its foreignness frightening and threatening. I stand up, look out at the brick wall, the rusty railings, the dull grey sky; it has always been a prison sentence, never a view. I close the curtain in anger and resentment, switch on the light and the TV. The news: there are demonstrations; a bomb has exploded somewhere. I do not quite understand, as if it is all in a language I have forgotten.

I suggest coffee but he does not want it. Instead, he comes over and stands before me, stares as he takes off his jacket and shirt, lets his trousers and pants fall to the floor, holds me with his eyes as he kicks them away. I look up from his groin to his stare: his expression is so painful that I am afraid to speak, to ask what is wrong. Then, as if suddenly released, I grasp his buttocks and pull his prick, his body, into my mouth as deep as I can.

He has fallen onto the bed. His eyes are closed; he trembles and breathes as if he were dying and I was the one who had killed him. I watch for a moment, then open my jeans, straddle his chest and force myself into him. He chokes, but does not push me away.

The television voices go on and on. As I open my eyes I realise I have been asleep. In alarm I sit up, but he is there, in the chair. He looks at me: I think he smiles. I lie down again, sink back into the warmth, protected by his presence, the duvet, the room.

He makes tea, turns down the television, comes to sit on the bed. 'Sleep well?' But he is not interested in the answer; there is a weight within him, the weight of something he has to say.

'Do you like doing it with me?' he eventually asks. The question surprises me; I tell him yes. He says nothing. I wait. 'I can't do it often enough,' he half-grins in apology. 'You're the first person who hasn't complained, who wants to do it with me all the time. The others . . . they wanted to talk or fall in love or tell me what to do. You just want to do it.' He looks thoughtful, serious. 'I don't want to stop. I want to do it again. *Now*.' He doesn't move, but I feel my own reaction, look at the black trousers that cover his. 'I want to do everything.' Everything? 'Everything,' he insists. 'Whatever there is to do. Do you know what I mean?' I nod and an impression, vague and formless, enters my mind, shimmering with fear and attraction.

But does he understand? Carefully, gently, afraid of asking the question or making the statement that might scare him away, I talk about what is possible, what others have done. He listens and I watch his expression as a yachtsman his compass – too much in the wrong direction and he frowns; when I am on course his eyes open wider. Thus I learn he does not desire ropes or chains, blows or hurts, insults or humiliation. Nor does he want to dress up, to parade in someone else's uniform or costume. It is the body itself that enthralls him, its reactions and limits, how far

95

one can penetrate, what makes the penis swell, what causes each sensation.

He waits until I have finished, then throws himself on me, his lips crashing into mine, his hands kneading my back, burrowing under my shirt. For a moment it is like the first time. I can only yield, not take part, then I feel a rush so violent that it is almost anger and I push him off, roll on to him; and we fight for dominance as our mouths scrape each other's necks, and our hands and knees and feet kick off each other's clothes. I win because I am heavier, and for a moment I lie across him, see his flushed and eager face, his thin body with its few muscles and scattering of dark hairs, and I want less to make love with him than to be him. I fall and try to enter him with not just my mouth and prick, but with all my flesh, all my weight.

We fought and attacked and resisted like samurai, Greek wrestlers, heroes in war. We lie here panting, two duelling stags exhausted but not defeated, the noise of our breathing filling the room. I entered him again, tried to pierce with my seed not just his body but his heart, yet despite all my efforts, my fury and lust, we are as apart from each other as we were before. I will not accept this separation which defies my will; I grab him and pull him to me; he responds as urgently, and we move over and against each other with undiminished energy but greater cunning, knowing that the lust, the aggression and desire, has been freed from our groins and now lurks in every cell of our bodies. This love-making mocks, intimidates and challenges.

The radio plays quietly; the television has long since closed down. He sits up in bed, wearing an old sweater of mine, as I prepare another meal. He is in the mood to talk again, asks about the others who live in the house. I hardly know them, I say shortly; some I have never seen. Others have families and friends and jobs, yet stay here for years; when I pass them in the corridor, I no longer make the effort to smile. 'And the landlord?' I don't remember him; he is only a name on a cheque.

I want to know about the boy who played football, what kind of a person he was, what his body was like. His description is vague, tells me little more than they 'did it' once or twice a week. 'He was a bit funny, though. He never wanted to come. He used to get mad if it lasted less than an hour.'

'What happened? Why did you stop?'

'He got nicked.'

It takes me a moment to recognise the expression. 'And the girl?'

He shrugs and tells me even less.

Coming back from the bathroom he hands me an envelope. 'Is this you?' It's the giro. 'We're going to need it,' he says.

I look down and see that his face is red and there are tears in his eyes. He makes frantic signs that tell me not to stop; I grasp his head again and push and push. What I feel is not my held breath but his choking, not my melting but his struggling for air. I remember taking him in my mouth, how I always want more than he can give. I push harder, harder, and his grunts are the sounds of my orgasm.

The picture wobbles and there is faint smell of burning from the back of the set. Annoyed, I switch it off.

It becomes a contest to see who can make the other come. I resist and resent the explosion that threatens to destroy me, try to hold it back with clenched fists and face tight with anger, but there is nothing I can do; I will lose again.

We have no food. I refuse to go out. I sign the giro and give it to him, together with a list of the shopping we need. After he leaves, I believe even less he will come back.

A noise startles me. I raise my head from the bed and see him turn on the television, put packets and cans away. When he has finished, he wants to have a shower. I tell him no, then lift him and place him on the bed, lick him all over, lick him clean, lick him dry.

He arches his back, splays out his limbs, demands that I push his legs still further apart. The pain in his muscles is

97

reflected in his grimace. We are both dissatisfied; to me it is gymnastics, nothing more, to him a failed experiment.

We wants an erection that will last for ever. I take a shoelace and pull it tight until the flesh goes purple and I fear the protruding veins will burst. 'Now make me come!' he orders; 'make me come!' when I hesitate. I take hold of him, but it is like rubbing leather: the feeling has gone. I close my eyes and when I hear him groan and feel the liquid spattering into my mouth, I am afraid to taste and discover it is blood. It is only sperm; I am relieved but he is disappointed, for his prick is already shrinking and loosening its bond.

He would do anything for me, to me, that I asked. But it would mean little to either of us, for it is his body I want, his own sensations he needs. So we go on, he leading, I following, scarcely aware of each step we take.

The television has finally broken down. I miss its light, its endless images.

He wants more; he always wants more than I can give. 'Your hand,' he begged, 'your hand.' At last I yielded and, trembling more than he, let him guide it in. He cried, silently, tears overflowing, and looked at me with what I could only understand was pain and longing. Now he lies exhausted and I stare at his body and I stare at my hand, thinking of what I have done, of what I could have done, and my emotions are blank.

In the half-light I stare at the curtain and remember the world outside, the pavement and street, the people and buses and cars that pass. Dogs sniff there; litter is blown; children cry. Traffic growls, shops yawn. Buildings glare at each other and threaten to topple. The window should not exist, should be solid wall; the glass and the curtain make us too vulnerable, too open to the winds and the wrath of the world. Even the corridor worries me, the stairs up and the passage that takes us to the bathroom. Behind each door is a hostile face, an accusing voice.

'If I died, would you die with me?' he asks. I look at him uncertainly, not sure what to say.

I have dreamed of my parents. They were dressed in Edwardian costume and my mother offered me tea. My father asked about my studies and gave me advice. I did not understand and he repeated his words.

He lies across the bed. I kneel at his head and we kiss, my eyes open, taking in the strange angle of his body. He stops and whispers he loves me. This time I know I have heard. I have nothing to say, but I hope he never tells me again.

I come back from a shower and realise that the room stinks, that the sheets are dirty with semen and sweat. He sprawls on the chair, reading a book. It seems as if he has always been there; I cannot remember how I lived before he came, how I would live if he went. He is part of my body, the meaning of my life, my soul, my albatross. I look down at his body, the mess of his hair, his pale and spotted skin, the ugly jumble of flesh in his groin, the awkward knees and feet. I wonder what his attraction was, what it still is. I want to be alone again, but I do not want him to leave. I cannot live without him and will no longer live with him.

I lean over. He drops the book and reaches for me, rubbing gently and delicately until I am hard. Then his other hand guides mine to his thighs; he looks up as I let it rest there.

We make love more slowly than ever before. In the middle he asks if there is anything wrong. I start to say no, then tell him I think it'll soon be the last time. He seems to understand.

MAYBE

Dave Royle

Even now, Roland could remember those balmy summer nights
  Even now, Geoffrey could remember
  Even now, Jeffrey could remember those balmy
  Even now
  Even now, he could remember those balmy summer nights.
Nights when the warm Spanish air hung thick round his tanned
shoulders – thick with the perfume of jasmine and the promise of
sweet, stolen passion by the vineyards. He could recall, as if it
were yesterday, his first sight of Desmond
  his first sight of Brad
  his first sight of Scott – that magnificently chiselled physique,
surging with masculine power and yet, at the same time,
somehow shockingly vulnerable. That shaggy mane of sun-
bleached hair! Those penetrating blue eyes that reminded Jeffrey
. . . that reminded him of the tempestuous depths of the sea, wash-
ing against the rocks below them. He had known at once that here
was the real thing – that magical moment, caught between dream
and reality, and . . .

The doorbell rang. Steven usually ignored it, especially
when he was working. Generally it was only someone for
the girl in the flat upstairs, who laid claim to mysterious
French origins. She, in turn, was laid by a fairly constant
stream of gentlemen callers, doing their bit for the spirit of
the Entente Cordiale and her housekeeping budget.

Steven might have been more enthusiastic about

answering the bell if Fifi's visitors had looked more interesting. He sometimes wondered if he should suggest going into partnership with her. Combining some of the exotic clothes he'd seen her wearing with some of the more bizarre pieces of leather in his own wardrobe, they could cater for quite a range of tastes.

The bell rang again. Fifi's customers usually lost their nerve if they had to ring twice. It must be for him.

It was Paul, who was wearing a shapeless plastic mac and a battered, discoloured stetson. Raindrops quivered along the rim of the hat and fell, one by one, onto his nose. They reminded Steven of condensation falling on the cistern above the urinals at the tube station. One day, the ticket collector had jerked him off there. While the older man had pulled frantically on his cock, Steven had gazed silently at his own smudged reflection in the dirty tiles, and water from the cistern had fallen in freezing drops onto his head.

'Get that kettle on,' Paul said grimly. He walked past Steven and began to climb the stairs.

'You're soaking!'

'Slightly. Christ, it's August! I mean, bloody *August*!'

'Never mind,' Steven said, as they entered the shabby living room. 'I'll make you a nice cup of tea.'

'I thought you'd never offer.' Paul removed his hat and raincoat with an extravagant flourish, sending water flying around him. 'Weren't you spending yesterday cleaning this place?'

'I did,' Steven called from the kitchen.

'It's hard to believe.' Pushing a pile of women's magazines to one side, Paul threw himself down on the sofa and lit a cigarette.

'Must you?' Steven said sharply, as he re-entered the room.

'You haven't given up *again*!'

'At least I make the effort. You might be a little thoughtful.'

'It's very difficult. You give up so often . . .'

'At least I try!'

'Oh, have one for God's sake! You can't be expected to be

101

virtuous and cope with an English summer at the same time. It's not good for the soul.'

'You'll be the death of me,' Steven said, lighting his first cigarette in twenty-four hours. Immediately he felt sick, but carried on smoking.

His mother had made him a chocolate cake. They had some with their tea, sitting at the table by the window. He shifted his typewriter, papers and magazines.

'What are you working on now?' Paul asked.

'Another story for Gayswoon.'

'They've asked for another?'

'They loved the last one,' Steven said, defensively.

'Still calling you Hank Thrashley, are they?'

'I'm afraid so.'

'I can't imagine you in pink.' Paul leaned back in his chair and smiled.

'Eh?'

'The Barbara Cartland of Gay Romance.'

They stared silently through the window, watching rain fall monotonously on the grey roofs of Camberwell. The windows of the fish bar across the road were steamed up. Endless queues of slow-moving cars and buses passed backwards and forwards. The spray of water sent up by their wheels soaked the old newspapers littering the edge of the pavements. Pedestrians moved sluggishly through the rain, their heads bowed towards the glistening, dirty paving stones. Their faces looked hollow and tired, motionless with passive anger.

'Will it *ever* stop?'

'I'll give it two weeks,' Steven said, matter-of-factly. 'Then I'm off to Australia House.'

'Oh, I say that every year!'

'Well, I don't.'

'You wouldn't get into Australia – you're not a brain surgeon.'

Steven sighed. 'Why didn't I do the brain surgery option in the fourth form?'

'Because you liked the sound of domestic science.'

'Two sodding years spent trying to make shortbread. I've never liked it since.'

'I spent two years trying to make an apron in need-lework. By the time I'd finished it I'd grown so much it didn't fit.'

'That's liberal comprehensive education for you,' Steven said, blowing a stream of cigarette smoke at the window. There was a brief pause. 'Sydney's supposed to be wild.'

'Who?'

'The place.'

'It's hard to imagine anything called Sydney being wild.'

'Full of hunky, sun-tanned brain surgeons.'

'I couldn't cope!'

'I could,' Steven said.

Again a pause, as threads of rain, like strings of glass beads, cut diagonally across the window.

'I've had enough of this.'

'That makes two of us,' Paul said.

'My washing's still out in the yard. Spent all morning doing it, bent over the bath . . .'

'Waiting for the plumber to arrive?'

'With his big tool . . .'

'That's it!' They laughed together.

'I can't even be bothered to fetch it in.'

'It'll ruin your jockstraps.'

'Why?'

'They stretch,' Paul explained. 'They never go back to their original shape. It happened to mine in the Canaries. I went swimming in the pool with just a jock on; when I came out the straps were hanging down to my knees!'

'Fuck it. I can't be bothered. Who cares?'

They were quiet again for a few moments.

'What time is it?' Steven asked eventually.

'Two thirty.'

'God, it drags . . .'

'I've even run out of cigarettes.'

'I might not even give it two weeks.'

'Have you got any cigarettes?'

'I told you – I've given up.'

The rain was falling even harder. Through the window, the world was a blur of formless, grey blotches.

'You never did tell me about the Canaries.'

'Seems like a bloody dream now,' Paul said. 'But it was only three weeks ago.'

'So you had a good time.'

'It was wonderful!'

'Well – tell me about it!'

'It was paradise after this dump.'

'I'm sure it was!'

'Paradise.'

'I hope you behaved yourself.'

Paul looked momentarily nervous. 'Well,' he said, 'I was careful. You have to be, these days.'

'I suppose so.'

'Mind you, you wouldn't believe what's still going on in the bars!'

'Really?'

'Jesus!'

'What sort of things?'

'Back rooms – everything!'

Steven sighed. 'Holiday mentality, I suppose,' he said.

'Exactly.'

Steven leaned forward and pressed his nose against the cold glass of the window. 'Still, ' he said, 'I couldn't half do with going mental for a week or so . . .'

'Actually,' Paul said, quietly, 'I wasn't as careful as I should have been . . .'

Steven looked at him. 'You didn't go in the back rooms?'

'Once or twice.'

'My God!'

'Well . . .' Paul seemed uneasy.

'You didn't get fucked, did you?'

'Once or twice.'

'Christ!'

'I know, I know . . . but at the time you don't want to think about . . . being sensible. All you're aware of is that there are lots of gorgeous bodies writhing around in the dark.'

'Well, you *hope* they're gorgeous bodies.'

'Yeah, well. It's the noises. The panting and moaning – the sucking noises . . .'

'Stop it! I'll get a hard on.'

104

'There you are, you see,' Paul said. 'You understand. I just didn't want to know about all that at the time. I just strolled in there – well, fell in, really. You can't see much.'

'And that was that, as they say.'

'I was being screwed before I knew it.'

'Paul!'

'I know.'

'You're a disgrace.'

'I was fucked three times.'

'Three!'

'I made sure it was OK,' Paul said, hurriedly.

'But *three*!'

'You're only twenty-four once.'

'That doesn't mean much in the dark,' Steven said.

Paul snatched a sheet of paper out of the typewriter. 'What's this?' he asked.

'It's the new story.'

'You can't have a hero called Roland!'

'I've already decided that.'

'Jeffrey's marginally better – so long as it's spelt with a J.'

'I've decided that, too.'

'Mind you,' Paul said, disparagingly, 'it's still pretty dire.'

'Thanks. I'm leaving the names till the end, or I'll never finish it.'

'You're very clever. I wouldn't know where to start.'

'I'm beginning to think *I* don't,' Steven said.

'You should write a story based on my holiday.'

'You're joking! Gayswoon doesn't want to know about back rooms and jockstraps.'

'It wasn't *all* like that,' Paul protested. He jumped up. 'Listen, I must be off. I have to meet Joe in twenty minutes.'

'I thought he sailed off to be a porn star in the States.'

'Decided it was too risky.'

Steven nodded. 'So it's still going on then, is it?'

'Off and on,' Paul said. 'He fucks like a dream!'

'So California's loss is yours and Battersea's gain.'

'They don't call him the Power Station for nothing!'

Steven laughed. 'Do they?'

'No. I just made it up.'

Steven closed his eyes tightly. ' *"The raindrops against the window panes sounded like thousands of pins dropping and scattering across a marble floor in a monastery."* '

'Pardon?'

'I just made it up.'

'I tell you, it's flashes of inspiration like that one that sets you apart.'

Steven felt flattered. 'Do you think so?'

'Without question.'

'I'm so bored, Paul.'

'I know. Get yourself a man. No, on second thoughts, don't. They've never done you much good, have they?'

'I don't need a man,' Steven said emphatically.

Paul looked at his friend. He was very handsome, in a rather tired kind of way. His eyes were blue, though not remarkably so. His hair was light brown – lots of people had light brown hair. They had been friends for more than ten years, and in all that time Paul had never seen Steven's cock. Steven had seen his – once, when they were sharing a flat in Belsize Park. Paul often remembered the occasion, though he suspected that Steven had long forgotten all about it. It was one freezing evening in January: Paul was pissed and penniless. He wanted to go out to a bar – to find someone and go home with him and forget all about unemployment and poverty – but there was no money, and, anyway, it was cold outside. The flat was warm and comfortable.

In his drunken stupor, he'd formulated a fantasy – that Steven had suddenly burst into his room and fucked him hard on the table. He remembered standing naked by the kitchen door, swaying drunkenly while Steven moved about the room, absorbed in preparing the evening meal.

'Put it away,' Steven had said, scarcely looking up at him. There had been a note of irritation in his voice. That had been the end of it: Paul had staggered off to bed without any dinner, disappointed and frustrated. He had wanted to have a wank, but instead had fallen into a heavy, disgruntled sleep, alone and cold.

He had never thought about Steven in such a sexual way since that evening. It seemed strange now, but it was even stranger that they'd been friends for so long and he'd never seen his cock. There were other things he didn't know about Steven.

'I must go,' Paul said.

'All right.'

'Still coming Friday?'

'Yeah – maybe.'

'Cheer up. The weather's the same through everyone's window.'

Steven smiled. 'I know,' he said.

Paul put on his coat and hat. He wanted to give Steven a big hug, but they only did that at Christmas or on their birthdays. He loved Steven.

Steven walked with him to the door. The rain had stopped; it was almost sunny. A group of workmen emerged from the fish bar. One of them – a youth with straggly blond hair and overalls – glanced at Steven and Paul.

'I saw him first!'

Steven laughed. 'Carry on,' he said.

'Take care, Steve.'

'I will. See you soon.'

They touched each other lightly on the shoulder, and then Paul turned away and hurried off to the bus stop.

'If only our time together wasn't so short! If only we could hold each other for just a day – just an hour – longer! My love!' Scott pulled Jeffr . . . Scott pulled him towards his powerful chest, and felt that same, familiar surge of helpless devotion. He was power-less to resist. He just kept murmuring over and over again, as if in harmony with the mysterious murmuring of the sea behind them, 'I love you . . . I love you . . . I love you.' In their hearts they knew the agony of imminent separation, the hideous tragedy of their inevitable parting. They knew, too, that their plans for the future were merely hopeless dreams. They would never meet again. Their lives were like two speed-boats on the blue sea, whiz-zing away in opposite directions. Their mutual love was a fragile sailing boat, about to be smashed on the rocks of reality for-ever . . .

No, whizzing wasn't right. Fifi was fucking in the flat

upstairs. Steven could hear the faint sound of a creaking bed and a man panting.

The sunshine had lasted for ten minutes, and now the sky had darkened again and a few spots of rain were falling against the window. Steven was niggled. He didn't like the idea of love as a whizzing speedboat. Technology was one thing – his story about gay passion at a computer exhibition had been a roaring success for Gayswoon – but a whizzing speedboat was something different.

Paul had been looking tired, though it seemed to Steven that he grew more handsome with each passing year.

He stared at the page of typescript in front of him. Could he somehow have his two lovers wandering round a monastery? The marble floors would be OK with the Spanish location, but why should anyone be dropping pins in a Spanish monastery? He felt confused. He couldn't think of one good reason.

He got up from the desk and picked up his leather jacket from the arm of the sofa. Then he hesitated. It was wet outside, but it wasn't cold. He threw the jacket down on the sofa and went into the hall. He took his denim jacket down from the coat-hook. No. It *was* wet outside, and getting wetter, and it wasn't *that* warm. He stood motionless for a moment in the doorway. Fifi had finished fucking. He heard her visitor leave, re-entering the outside world with an embarrassed, cover-up cough. The light in the centre of the living-room ceiling swayed as Fifi padded to her bathroom. His grey anorak would be the most sensible thing.

The tube smelt of wet clothes. Steven pretended to be asleep, though he could never quite trust himself to keep his eyes shut when the train pulled into a station. He mustn't miss the stop.

He thought about Paul again. They were old friends, and friendships endure over time and space, so it was said. It occurred to him that he didn't know where Australia House was. He felt distinctly uneasy – uncomfortable with himself. It was silly – he should have checked before he left home.

He opened his eyes. A hunky clone was sitting opposite, watching him, an intense look in his eyes. Steven noticed how he spread his legs fractionally wider apart, almost imperceptibly, when his look was acknowledged. Steven shut his eyes again.

There was still that feeling of unease, growing stronger. As the train stopped at Embankment, and Steven got out, he realised that it had nothing to do with wondering where Australia House was. It was something more disturbing. If he left England, he might never see Paul again, and he couldn't decide if he cared or not. There seemed to be no clear answer to anything any more. The rails clicked and hummed softly as he stood on the platform, wondering.

THE SOLITARY COLLECTOR

Paul Davies

Unseen, unobstructed, I work my way through the streets of the city. Observing, recording. Watching the world in its daily activity, looking on as others rush about in the pursuit of their businesses and desires. Whilst I, unemployed, pursue my own private occupation. I move around, occasionally pausing in shop-fronts and coffee-bars, libraries and galleries, as I go about the task of adding to my collection.

Today has not been very successful as yet. It is raining hard and there are few people around. I have been unable to find a single new item – which is most unusual, and somewhat disappointing. Although I suppose I have no right to grumble, given the substantial size of the collection. There are, I am sure, many less dedicated collectors who would be satisfied with what I would term a bad day – a day, that is, on which less than four new articles are acquired. It is only half past two as yet, so there is still time for me to find a little something or other. Even if I do fail, I can rest content in the knowledge that mine is almost certainly the largest collection of its kind in the country, if not the entire world – I suppose I would be entitled to a place in the *Guinness Book of Records* if I wanted one.

I began collecting at the somewhat early age of nine – I believe I was the first in my class to do so. And although several of the others probably started shortly after I did, none, I think, took up the hobby with my enthusiasm and dedication. In fact, so keen was I on collecting that I really don't know how I managed to find time to do anything else. By my fourth year at secondary school it had become an obsession – it was as if I was in the grip of some strange religion. Although I am somewhat less zealous now, my faith is still as firmly rooted, and it is with some considerable pride that I look back on my schooldays, since it was then that the foundations of my collection were laid.

By the time I left school at fifteen – I was not academically-minded and had not been known as a hard worker; I believe my teachers were rather glad to see the back of me – I had a collection which numbered just over three thousand separate items, each recorded, by my own special system of notation (which I will explain in a moment), in a catalogue. Had my school-fellows known about it, they would have been most envious, I am sure, but I preferred to keep my activities to myself. Indeed, I went to great lengths to ensure that my contemporaries did not get their hands on my secret. The most remarkable thing about the collection is probably the fact that, although I have spent most of my life in the business of acquiring new specimens, and although it occupies a place in my thoughts for at least twelve hours in every twenty-four, its existence is completely unknown to anyone else. You are privileged, dear reader, very privileged, to be the first to learn of my life's secret work. I trust that you will not abuse the information you are about to be given, and will treat my confession with the respect you would desire from others who learn of *your* obsessions and clandestine hobbies.

I am about to reveal, for the first time, the nature of my unique collection. But before I do so, perhaps I should add a few words of warning. As with many enjoyable activities, there are some people who, for one reason or another – be it moral, religious, or out of mere ignorance and prejudice – find it objectionable and demand that others be prevented from seeking pleasure in this fashion. If you are such a person, then you may well demand the destruction of my collection – so stop reading here! If you are not such a person – and I would hope that most of my readers have liberal and open minds – then please feel free to proceed.

111

I collect images and impressions. A common pursuit perhaps, but the images I collect are not of the same order as those involved in such pastimes as portrait and sculpture collecting or, at the other end of the market, the accumulation of picture postcards or pop magazines. No. Such hobbies strike me as being rather passive and purposeless. I am not content with amassing a pile of pictures in whose creation I have played no part. I need to have a hand in the making of the images – I suppose there must be a touch of the artist in me. The images that I have collected are those forged in my own imagination. They are images of people: people in a variety of positions and places. They are recorded as they fell upon my mind, and I have fixed them in my memory with the white cement of ejaculation. You see, my hobby is masturbation, and my collection is of those people fortunate enough to have found a place in my onanistic fantasies.

To date, thirty-nine thousand, two hundred and seventy-eight people have been so favoured – rather an impressive number, don't you think? Particularly when you consider the fact that the collection has not even reached its probable half-way point: I have been collecting now for some twenty-seven years and, God willing, I hope to reach eighty thousand before my death. I am afraid I have had to abandon my early ambition to get into six figures – alas, how easily frustrated are the dreams of youth! Some of the people in the collection are known to me personally: family, acquaintances, friends of acquaintances. Others are people whose names are household words: public figures, television personalities, actors and models. But the majority are faces without names: bodies unknown, given meaning only by the labels I attach to them and by their place in the collection.

Of course, keeping nearly forty thousand images in one's mind is a near-impossible task, and I am assisted here by the catalogue which I have kept meticulously throughout my collecting life. I began recording collected specimens when I was ten, and so was able to note down all the previous images which were still quite fresh in my memory – indeed, the only thing missing in relation to the first twenty-six items is the date. I have kept to the same basic system of notation since my youth – adding refinements to it here and there, but never subtracting from it.

Immediately after collection – or rather, as soon as possible afterwards, for, as I am sure you will appreciate, there are many occasions on which immediate cataloguing is impractical – I write down the details of the new specimen on a record card. This is divided into three sections. In Section A, I record the factual details: name (if known) of the specimen, its physical characteristics, the time and place of capture, etc. In Section B, I record the nature of my masturbatory fantasy. And in Section C, I write an appreciation and evaluation of the new addition. At the head of each card I write the specimen's number, and it is then retained in one of the many files that fill my bedsit.

An example:

SECTION A

SPECIMEN No. 35486
NAME: Unknown
SEX: Male   RACE: Italian
AGE: 17-18   HEIGHT: 5'5"
BUILD: Slim   EYES: Hazel
HAIR: Jet black
DRESS: Tight white jeans, blue and white striped tee-shirt, gold crucifix on neck chain.
DISTINCTIVE FEATURES: Brilliant white teeth; a seductive, mischievous smile; attractive birth-mark on left temple.
PLACE OF CAPTURE: Leicester Square
DATE OF CAPTURE: 8/6/74   TIME: 11.17 a.m.

SECTION B

He is eating a vanilla ice-cream: his tongue licks slowly, revealing his beautiful teeth. He comes to me, removes my trousers and underpants, and then places the cone – still

113

bursting full with ice-cream – on to my erect penis. He pushes it right on, and then proceeds to eat it. I caress his head, fondling his long, smooth ebony hair. Soon the ice-cream is eaten, and the Italian boy has a mouthful of vanilla-flavoured sperm.

SECTION C

A choice specimen. Both reality and fantasy in the top grade. Judging by the bulge in his white jeans, the ice-cream boy may well be worth collecting again.

Rather impressive, don't you agree? I'm sure that other people's collections do not contain many specimens as exquisite as this.

Some more details about my notation system: in Section C above, I mention that the specimen concerned might be worth re-collecting at a later date (a task, alas, which remains unaccomplished.) When a specimen is collected for a second, third or thirtieth time, a record card is made out in the same way, but is attached to the earlier card with a letter added after the file number. Thus, if I had captured the ice-cream boy a second time, the second card would be headed 34586(a). There are a number of re-collected specimens in the catalogue, and some are quite regular acquisitions. For example, there is Terry Hodges, a schoolfellow of mine, who still lives in the same street as he did when I first collected him twenty-seven years ago. Terry entered the collection as Specimen No. 15, when he was a boy of eight. He is now middle-aged, fat, bald, and Specimen No. 15(rj). Terry has been collected some five hundred and four times – which works out at an average of eighteen point six recurring per year. I am rather fond of Terry!

Mr Hodges, however, is something of an exception. Most specimens are collected once and once only. I will describe to you some of my favourite examples, but before I do so, I think I ought to outline some of the principles of the art of onanism which I believe to be essential to any understanding of the subject.

Firstly, dedication. Onanism is a total way of life, and a true onanist is devoted to his art above all other things – it is not something for mere week-end wankers. So dedicated to my craft am I that I have resisted the temptation of sexual contact with other beings, studiously keeping myself pure. And when I talk about the avoidance of contact with others, I mean this as an absolute rule – even furtive frottage is out of the question. All contact, however clandestine, is forbidden.

Secondly, the true masturbator is not content with collecting images from magazines in the comfort and security of his bedroom. No. Live specimens are necessary. This entails venturing into exposed and often dangerous habitats: the crowded bus, the public bar, the busy street – this is the domain of the true collector.

The collection of live specimens is a difficult business, and the ability to succeed in problematic environments is what distinguishes the professional from the merely gifted amateur. It is absolutely essential to master the art of collecting specimens without arousing their attention. A specimen in the process of being captured must remain unaware of the thoughts, intentions and hand movements of the collector. In my whole onanistic career, I have been detected only once, and that was nearly twenty-five years ago. It happened when I was still a novice in the art: Mr Jenkins, my English teacher, turned rather suddenly from the blackboard, where he had been writing out a passage for comprehension, and found that my attention was focused elsewhere. I suppose the rather hasty withdrawal of my offending hands alerted him to the nature of my distraction. 'Play with yourself in your own time, boy, not during my lessons!' he shouted. My school-fellows found this rather amusing and mocked me from that day on – I was christened *The Wanker* and *The Dreaded Hands*. But I was never very close to my contemporaries, and didn't regard their opinions as being of much worth.

But what Mr Jenkins and the entire class did not realise was that, at the very moment of his shout, the English master had become Specimen No. 737(c) in the collection.

Single-minded dedication, the courage and ability to collect in adverse environments, and the skill to avoid detection: these are the three cornerstones of the onanist's art.

My collection is vast not only in size but also in range. I collect both men and women, of any age and of any race. I do not discriminate against anybody – I even include monopeds and the mentally handicapped. They range across eight decades in terms of age, the eldest being eighty-five. My desire can be channelled anywhere, so subservient is it to that greater desire – the urge to collect.

Now let me show you the pride of my collection. My prize exhibit, a veritable specimen amongst specimens!

Well, perhaps not just yet. Maybe I should show you some lesser items first, by way of preparation, as a foreplay to the *magnum opus*. After all, building up and sustaining tension is an integral part of my craft: one must learn to control the climax.

My earlier talk of the skill necessary to avoid being discovered reminds me of a recent acquisition, captured in circumstances that, I am sure you will agree, were hardly conducive to my operations.

Friday evening at six o'clock, sitting on a north-bound tube train on the Northern Line, Edgware branch: I was not able to sit down, so crowded was the carriage. Seated immediately in front of me was a young gentleman engrossed in the sports pages of *The Standard*. His looks were, I suppose, undistinguished, although his nose would not have been out of place on a Hollywood actor or a Parisian model. His clothes were the very height of fashion: a well-cut Italian suit with an exquisite pale blue silk tie, and expensive soft leather shoes (although I do recall noticing a rather nasty scratch on the toe of the left one). But it was the situation more than the gentleman that aroused my acquisitive interests: here was a juicy specimen, ripe for the plucking!

The prospective specimen put down his paper and looked straight ahead, adopting the blank, semi-conscious stare of the habitual commuter. From his dress and manner I guessed that he would probably alight at Hampstead, so I calculated that I would have a maximum of ten stops in which to accomplish capture.

116

I suppose there must be a touch of the magician in me, for one of the skills that I have taught myself is the use of the left hand as a means of distracting attention from the activities of the right. And so, in order to protect myself from the unwelcome gaze of fellow-passengers, I proceeded to lend my left hand to the performance of activities which are normally carried out only in private. By which I mean the picking of one's nose, the biting of one's nails and (most repellent of all) the smelling of one's armpits. Within five mintues, before the train had reached Goodge Street, I had succeeded – every eye in the carriage studiously avoided looking in my direction.

Having thus accomplished this diversion, I was free to proceed with the next phase of the operation. My right hand was moved into the collecting position by means of a specially designed, bottomless trouser pocket – one of my own little inventions. Then, slowly, I began collecting, taking care not to make any sudden movements that might alarm the prey. As we left Warren Street I increased the pace slightly to about sixty s.p.m. (Another of my notational terms – it stand for 'strokes per minute'). But no sooner had I settled into a steady and relaxed rhythm than disaster struck.

The train jolted and I, having no hand free to support myself, was thrown onto the floor. I was helped to my feet by none other than the young gentleman in the Italian suit, for which I both thank and curse him. Curse him, because his action meant that collector and would-be specimen had come into physical contact with each other. I thus had to abandon the attempt at capture.

However, since my hunting and gathering instincts were still very much aroused, I felt that I could not complete the journey without making some acquisition. So, when I was on my feet, I faced away from my assistant and began to collect the person now in front of me. I had made the decision to do this before I had even seen the person concerned. (This is a procedure that I adopt from time to time, and it is known as "blind collecting". To distinguish specimens collected in this fashion in the catalogue, the capital letter "B" is added after the specimen number on the record card – for example, 21432B.) Now, whilst not measuring up to the quality of the previously intended specimen, the new one was not as unpleasant as some I have collected blindly. He was middle-aged, balding, with a ginger moustache; he wore jeans and a blue and red check shirt. He also had a bunch of keys hanging from his belt and an ear-ring in his right ear.

I could not afford to waste any more time. I quickly worked myself up to ninety s.p.m., and after little more than a minute I had cross the one hundred barrier. But then it seemed that disaster was about to strike me a second time. As the train slowed down to approach Euston, the specimen-designate made clear his intention to disembark. I was therefore obliged to increase my pace, which is a dangerous procedure. Normally I would not go above one hundred and fifteen s.p.m. when collecting on public transport, but on this occasion I had to climb the giddy and perilous heights of the upper one hundred and sixties.

Nonetheless, I succeeded. Specimen no. 38942B became a part of the collection at six twenty-three p.m., at the very moment when the doors of the train slid open to discharge the flow of weary commuters.

And now the time has arrived to tell you of the prize exhibit, the most stunning specimen in the whole gallery of my masturbatory fantasy. My most brilliant achievement, my *pièce de resistance*.

Again it was captured in a public place, and one more exposed than a carriage on an underground train. However, on this occasion there was no chance of the specimen escaping, since she was taking part in an elaborate and ancient ritual with a fixed pattern from which she could not deviate. And as her movements were set, I regulated mine accordingly. The occasion was a wedding. A wedding, moreover, of two rather famous personages. I, the uninvited guest, stood at the back of St. Paul's . . .

I am sorry to disappoint you, but I have just ejaculated – I hadn't realized how exciting story-telling could be. So I am afraid you will never know the details of how Lady Diana Spencer became Specimen No. 32,169 at the very moment she became the Princess of Wales.

This rainy afternoon has not been as fruitless as I feared it might be. There is now a new specimen in the collection. Yes, dear reader, that specimen is *you*. (And you thought you were in a position of safety? On the contrary, I can see you very clearly, very clearly indeed.) *You* are Specimen No. 39279B in the collection (or 39279B(a) if you are reading this a second time.) You are 39279B because you are collected blindly. I had little choice in the matter. I am sorry to tell you that you are not one of my most memorable acquisitions. Good enough though for a rainy afternoon.

ORANGES AND LEMONS

Peter Robins

At the base of a ramp that leads from the upper terraces Nurse Oliver hesitates.

'What path do you suggest sir? Left or right?'

'I've no preference. The middle will do as well as any . . .' As his invalid chair chews noisily through the deep gravel Lord Newham continues to mutter. To mutter testily would more accurately describe his tone. '. . . So? Where's my usual keeper?'

'You mean Nurse Charlie, sir? Indisposed with an un-explained stomach ache. You've got me this afternoon. The name's Oliver.'

Lord Newham grunts. Being certain that Oliver – in common with all members of staff – has been vetted for pol-itical reliability he lacks any impulse to chat. For Reggie Newham it seems less exhausting to contemplate the grey-gilt waters of the Thames. His affection for this particular river is more constant than any he can recall experiencing for either human or domestic animals. Mitch excepted. Reggie has enjoyed a life-long companionship with the Thames. Its surface mirrored him diving as a boy in darned underpants. He rehearsed each public speech at night with the ebbing tide for audience until all rallies were banned by promulgation at the end of the Urban War. Had his chair at this particular moment been nearer the towpath, he would have been able to peer among the nettles and dockleaves at his reflected face surrounded by a few white rags of hair.

He would have been as swift to note – as Nurse Oliver has – eyes more lacklustre than those of the Regional Controller himself.

Oliver – having pushed his charge to the lower balustrade – locks the brakes. He settles his elbows on the parapet and both men gaze silently at those promenading gently across the lawns below. Occasionally Lord Newham waves laconically towards some passing couple. Another resident accompanied by another nurse. An elderly woman shouts some commonplace about the daffodils and Reggie smiles. 'Tra la for the flowers in spring,' he growls but she is already out of earshot. Oliver's head shifts slightly, but Lord Newham is disinclined to expand on his comment. He has no wish to share with the nursing staff any recollection of those events which the daffodils stir in him. Every day of every year – but more intensely as the March winds ease – he relives the final skirmishes that bloodied London's streets with unsuccessful sacrifices. Six years – he calculates – almost to the week.

Nurse Oliver – turning to him – smiles. 'A really warm day at last.'

'The ducks over there would appear to be enjoying it.'

'But you're not?'

'There are less agreeable places than Richmond Hill on a March afternoon. I'd not quarrel with you about that, Oliver. But let's not pretend there aren't more pleasant surroundings than these.'

In a seemingly casual way Oliver squats. He begins to tuck in the tartan rug methodically, though there is no evidence that it is coming adrift. Reggie studies the young man, and notes the careful placing of Oliver's back to the balustrade and the river. He calculates that whatever Oliver is about to say cannot be filmed or recorded from camouflaged equipment on the Twickenham bank.

'Lord Newham? . . . Are you listening? Lord Newham, you ought to know I'm not what I appear to be.'

An irony perfected through decades of argument informs Reggie's glance and his reply: 'You stagger me. Or you would if I were walking. Not what you appear to be?

D'you know, I hadn't the haziest suspicion my six-monthly security check might be due. New technique, is it? The soft approach in a natural setting? Oliver, you Party Investigators pop up like blackheads. I presume you are a Security lackey. A former lavatory attendant perhaps – raised to the big time by a set of curious chances?'

Oliver is silent for a moment. Long enough for the Englishness of Reggie Newham to be lightly underlined. He's already quoted twice from a still popular Victorian operetta. Were it put to him that his international sympathies could threaten his regard for his own land, there's little doubt Reggie would snort and assert that he had always been as English as *Greensleeves* played on a tin whistle. Without further digression into Reggie's allegiances – for this is a brief story – let's hear Oliver's response. 'I am not . . . never have been . . . and bloody well never will be an Investigator.' He no longer fusses with the travelling rug. Unclenching his left palm for a second he discloses a two-toned metal badge: an orange and a lemon semi-circle.

Reggie Newham's eyes glance away more swiftly than a startled thrush and he surveys craft passing up and down the river. 'The fellow over there, Oliver . . . the one who appears to be a tourist in grey at the prow of that pleasure steamer . . . Who's he pointing his camera at? Is it us?'

He anticipates – correctly – that Oliver will turn to check. As he does so Reggie depresses a minute button on the pocket of his tunic.

'Can't be certain, Lord Newham, but I wouldn't think so. Look . . . about your regular nurse. You ought to know I laced Charlie's breakfast with laxative so I could be with you this afternoon. Just to put one question. This is not – repeat *not* – a Security Check. By Them . . . or Us. We agreed long ago it wouldn't be necessary. After all . . . your whole life's record speaks for itself, doesn't it?'

'Do save your breath, Oliver. Always supposing that is your name. If all this blether and boyscouting of yours is some prelude to sounding out my views on the Freedom Brigade, it's not on. Now . . . maybe you'd be so kind as to trundle me back to my suite. I'm quite happy to swallow my sedatives early today. Incidentally . . . I'm still a privileged citizen. My mini-cassette has been on Record for some minutes. Should you attempt . . .'

Oliver laughs disarmingly and does not move. 'I'm hardly the one to be blackmailing you, Lord Newham. I don't even need to worry about trusting you. I know I can! Even if I were dubious, I'll have gone to ground by sunset. Had some practice at that these past few years . . .'

Reggie gives no indication that he hears – let alone heeds – the young man's words. His eyes follow a swirl of starlings as they make for Teddington or Staines. Only when their individuality is lost in an amorphous smudge does he lose interest. When he speaks he does not look at Oliver. 'Sounds very brave. Not taking much of a risk, are you, if you're no more than a Party hireling here to test my reliability? . . . Say you're not. Maybe you are from the Freedom Brigade. What d'you want from me, eh? Lord Newham's no more than a performing seal. Think I don't know that just as well as the clones at Regional Hall? You're too late, Oliver. Years too late.'

Oliver perches himself deftly on the edge of the parapet, but does not interrupt. He judges that there will be a space between the old man's words into which he can insert argument and persuasion. He waits for that moment, content to let Reggie Newham's sigh be the prelude to small reminiscences.

'As for my life's record . . . all that's at Regional Hall too. Suitably edited, you understand. Decades of words . . . projects . . . ideals, I suppose one might say . . . all neatly subbed to a couple of paragraphs. As for the bits they've filleted out – the bones, eh? – I've had opportunity enough here to think back on them . . . in so far as the bloody sedatives allow. Tell you something, Oliver. I wasted the nineteen nineties, you know. O yes! Ten whole years frittered away between rallies and mourning friends who were clubbed down in the food riots. That's all yesterday now. Today . . . and tomorrow . . . I'm thinking of me. What's left of me. I'm old. I'm alone and . . . that's how it has to be. All my mates gone, Oliver . . . every lovable one hauled off

123

to Smithfield on a single ticket. I take it you are aware of what goes on at the old meat market?' Reggie pauses. Blows his nose raucously and squints up at the four o'clock sun.

Oliver does not speak until the reverberation of Reggie's last phrase is lost in the silent gardens. He then makes an observation very softly – uncertain of its effect. 'Mitch is very much alive and working with us.'

'Tricky young customer, aren't you, Oliver? My cousin was spattered over the ruins of Brixton, so you can stop playing the agent provocateur. Should have done your homework. There'll be photographs of me in the archives leaving the memorial service for Mitch . . .'

'Then it's as well you didn't know the coffin was empty, Lord Newham, or you might have been caught smiling. We'd snatched Mitch away. Poor bugger was a field hospital job but we sewed him up. He's been active with the Brigade for . . . best part of six years. I joined at much the same time.'

'I usually find con merchants amusing, Oliver, but I have to tell you you're beginning to irritate me. If it were true . . . that is . . . if Mitch or anyone else wants to indulge in Robin Hood antics . . . let 'em, I say. I'm through with hopes and possibilities. I exist. No, Oliver . . . hear me out. Let's consider why I'm permitted to go on existing. I'll tell you. I'm a waxwork trundled out to show any visiting Euro-delgates just how tolerant of reasonable dissent our London Regional goons are. That's what I am, Oliver: Reggie Newham . . . one of twelve lords a-lurching round the dear old Star and Garter on Richmond Hill. A kind of three-dimensional publicity poster, you might say. Don't look dismayed! I may babble heresy but I'm no menace to them. Not sufficient anyway to merit a Goodbye Pill. I imagine most Londoners suppose me dead already. Well I am . . . except for the odd ritual appearance at Regional Senate togged up in my Father Christmas kit to tickle the tourists. Scarlet and ermine, eh? Unlike Father Christmas, I haven't one useful gift for a living soul. Not one mouthful of hope . . . far less an extra dollop of soya sausage which would be twice as practical. Oliver lad . . . I've nothing to offer anyone . . . Now that's a lie! We privileged citizens get a supplementary issue of carrot toffees. Would you care for one?'

It's debatable whether Reggie is more intent on fumbling with his plastic carton or on assessing Oliver's reaction to what has just been said. Lord Newham is old, but a life in politics has produced a wary tactician. He notes the way Oliver bites his lower lip and the beginning of what could be tears.

'Breeze making your eyes water, eh? Treacherous, these March gusts. I confess they might have helped to get me going . . . and your tiresome idealism too. There's no denying it – I've over-excited myself. You'll just have to fix me a treble bromide after tea, Oliver, to restore my sweet acquiescence. More immediately though – young man – if you're refusing a toffee we might as well move on.'

Saying nothing, Oliver complies. He turns the chair and pushes steadily until this seemingly odd couple is shaded by the sticky-buds of a horse chestnut. Oliver applies the brakes a second time and pulls two smuggled cigarettes from his blousson before he speaks. Reggie Newham anticipates further persuasion.

'Have you considered how very much alive you are to all of us? We remember things you really achieved . . . not that garbage printed in the Distinguished Citizens' Register. You don't really imagine you can erase a life's work with irony – do you? We don't forget the marches you led for peace in Vietnam. Didn't you support gay people's rights in the seventies? Who demanded food for immigrants and gypsies after that? . . . Well then . . . who?'

Reggie Newham flicks away his half-smoked cigarette with obvious irritation. Just as swiftly Oliver retrieves it and – having nipped the end – buries it in his pocket. Reggie attempts to convey the sincerity of what he says by banging the flat of his hand on the arm-rest of his invalid chair.

'Just push me away from here. Let's move into the sunlight. And you listen to me, young Oliver, before you slip back to your friends over the rainbow. Tell them what I'm telling you for all I care. Don't give too much of yourself to any cause, Oliver. Take it from one who knows. O yes! I'd have done better fleshing out my middle years learning to live with someone . . . a person I once cared about . . . all their body stinks and their tantrums. I never noticed them . . . too bloody dazzled I was by noble banners. What's more I let myself be used. Don't try deluding yourself, Oliver. There's a rapacious hunger for figureheads gnawing its way through every cause. Give us heroes, eh? What makes you suppose your precious Freedom Brigade's any different? The fact that you're here proves my point. You've come head-hunting for another name to cheer up the troops. Go back to 'em, Oliver. Tell 'em it was an afternoon wasted. You've been sniffing round a corpse.'

Perhaps Oliver is temporarily thrown by this outburst. He is certainly silenced. Having finished his cigarette he buries the stub by circling it into the gravel with his toe. Reggie is amused – seemingly satisfied even – that he is pushed in silence among the patchwork beds of polyanthus towards an uneven pavement where the gardens end and a public road winds towards the top of Richmond Hill. At the corner they are forced to wait for a squad of Junior Patriots – not one more than ten years old – to march briskly past. Each child wears an identical white plastic battletop. The banner which precedes them depicts the London Regional Controller. More precisely it depicts his head haloed in sunbeams rising from an improbably blue Thames.

Reggie laughs. 'Study them, Oliver. Your rabble couldn't come up with a master-stroke like that, I'll bet. Politics elevated to instant folk myth, eh? From trashy fascist to a sun-god in his own lifetime. They must be hiring a good marketing man at Regional Hall. You must admit it's effective. Ordinary folk still need their gods and demons, eh?'

'Well we don't, Lord Newham. And we don't go for heroes either. All right . . . there are one or two whose life patterns we dig. It didn't take a weekend's workshop before we included your name on the list . . .'

'Stop this damn thing again immediately! Come on round here and fix my rug. And look at me while I ask you this. What have I to offer? I'm a husk . . . a dying grandpa on the ice floe.'

Oliver moves round but he ignores the rug and stands – arms folded – confronting Reggie. He answers with an urgency that suggests his time rather than his patience is limited.

'We need your experience. And the vision you've been denying this past hour. The fire isn't out, and you know it. You're a dissident – a rebel . . . and we both know that. All this piss you've been giving me can't douse one thing . . . you're a sexual rebel. Always have been. There's sod all for you in this . . . this clone factory that was once England. Unless you join us. Reggie Newham, you belong with us, my friend . . .'

'Oliver. Oliver . . . resistance work is for the young . . .'

'What's young? How old's your heart?' Oliver pulls two identical white tablets from his tunic. He places one in each of his palms and – with a nod – invites Reggie to examine them. 'Indistinguishable, eh? In my right hand your bromide – if you still insist on trotting back up the hill to the gargoyles' graveyard. But this – though you talk about it – you've probably never seen. Our friend the quadruple sedative – the Goodbye Pill. If you suppose I'm luring you on a trip to Smithfield you can always use it.'

'Could be powdered chalk though, Oliver – couldn't it? Wouldn't be much of a comfort, would it? They're none too gentle with Brigade sympathisers, I've heard.'

As he searches the old man's face Oliver glimpses – for the first time – the sign for which he has been waiting. Reggie's eyes twinkle as he speaks, and Oliver knows he must now put the question he has to ask. 'Will you come?'

Although Reggie hears the invitiation clearly, he is already considering how Mitch might look. While Oliver waits motionless, Lord Newham is already alone with Mitch and wondering what his cousin's reaction would be to the casual admission of an affection concealed under half a century's subterfuge. For some reason that he does not instantly analyse, an awareness of Oliver's face waiting for a response prompts a new thought. Reggie does not give a damn what his own cousin's reaction will be. 'I'm not leaving London, Oliver. Now see here . . . Why not trot back and tell your mates I do think of them plotting forays in their disused tube tunnels? Look . . . even when I'm not sedated I'm not so nippy on my feet as I used to be.'

'Without us you're dead. Let's stop fucking about. Give me just one valid reason why you need to go on breathing if I trundle you back to the funny farm.'

Seemingly oblivious of Oliver's increasing agitation Reggie stares beyond the budding trees to the distant Thames. The sun is obscured by cloud and the river is sludge grey. Oliver fingers his watch. Finally Reggie chuckles and – leaning forward – squeezes Oliver's scarred hand. 'If my contemporaries . . . better say my peers . . . are either gaga or collaborators, who can a man listen to but the young?'

Freeing his hand Oliver punches Reggie playfully on the chest. 'Let's go. Now.'

Along each side panel of the battered van the lettering is colourful rather than tasteful. Since the purpose of the graphic artist may well have been to evoke such a response in passers-by, she or he may be said to have been success-ful. *CLEMENTS FOR REMOVALS* is the subject of little or no comment this particular afternoon, at the far end of a cul-de-sac opposite the corner by which Reggie and Oliver have been tussling verbally.

Oliver – guiding the wheelchair into the brief, empty street – gives a thumbs-up. This is noted in the cracked driving mirror, but not by Reggie. When they reach the rear of the van both can hear the driver snoring. Not until Oliver unfastens the door does Reggie notice that a greasy cap obscures the driver's face. Only when he has been edged from his chair to the floor of the van does he have a moment to consider and voice further misgivings. 'What about this chair? We'll be missed in less than an hour, Oliver . . .'

128

Oliver replies by jutting his chin towards the interior. Reggie – peering a second time – freezes. What appears to be a mirror image of himself – looking so lifelike that it could still be warm to the touch – is propped against a coffin lid. Reggie cowers on the spread tarpaulin.

'Abducted yesterday, Lord Newham. Kept under sedation. Until three minutes ago when at long bloody last you saw sense.'

'No man can be that valuable, Oliver. Certainly I'm not. That poor soul had to die for me?'

'Save your liberal compassion. The poor soul's been an Assistant Investigator at Smithfield. His misfortune was being your weight and height. We have the services of a good make-up artist. I'll dump him back in the grounds. Right . . . we may not meet for some days. Travel safe.'

As Oliver speaks he drags the corpse past Reggie and into the wheelchair. With a wink that Reggie finds disturbing he slams the van doors and thumps twice. The driver removes his cap and flicks the ignition key. Reggie shouts over the noise of the engine: 'How do I know this coffin's not for me?' Whether Oliver hears the question is irrelevant. It is not he who answers.

'You don't. Could come in useful on a temporary basis if there's trouble down the road, Reggie.'

Reggie's reaction to the driver's turn of phrase and accent is extraordinary. He is convinced he might be on the edge of a seizure. His limbs tremble. His throat dries and his heart quivers like a leaf. He braces himself to turn, and then it seems to him that minutes must have passed before he has swivelled sufficiently to look at the driver. The face in the mirror is battered. Patched. Scarred. It is Mitch.

Reggie stammers: 'You've altered.'

Mitch laughs over his shoulder as he changes from bottom to second gear. 'Let's hope to Christ you have too.'

'You know, I'm still wondering if I've made an insane decision.'

'So what's new? Too much self-doubt was always your downfall, Reggie. Comes of having that middle-class mother, I always said.'

129

They both laugh as the van moves quickly across the Bridge of the Vigilant Patriots. For more than two centuries this graceful span of stones was known as Richmond Bridge. Reggie folds his top-coat into a pad and kneels directly behind his cousin. He wonders whether he ought to wait for an unexpected swerve along their route so that his arm might seem to slide accidentally along Mitch's shoulder.

'Reggie Newham. If you're going to bloody hug me, get on with it and don't have us off the road.'

The hair at Mitch's nape is more silver than auburn and yet it is as soft against Reggie's lips as he had always supposed it might be. After some moments Mitch eases himself forward.

'If you'd had fewer self-doubts years ago, our Reggie, you'd have got all the responses you needed. Did you fancy young Oliver?'

'Fancy him? Really! He can't be more than twenty-two or . . .'

'Good lad, though. Did the trick, eh? I picked him out. Forgotten how I looked at twenty-two, Reggie?'

'Of course! That was what I couldn't place! Thought of everything, haven't you? I suppose everything's fair in love and politics . . .'

Mitch shrugs but says nothing until they've skirted the walls of the Loyal School of Military Music. 'Right now, Reggie . . . and tomorrow . . . and the next day . . . we need practical heads and hands. Just put a final tick against all those doubts of yours, my old darling. We're not doing a touring show of Hamlet, see?'

The lights of an intersection are against them. Reggie sits back on his heels as the van slows. To one side of the tarmac ahead there's the hedged boundary of a playing field. Through the right-hand window Reggie could see – if he chose to look – a crumbled ragstone wall and then a disused church. The lights change and the van moves forward. It has barely cleared the intersection when – for no reason immediately discernible to Reggie – it swerves across the grass to lodge no more than a metre from the playing field gates.

Reggie grabs his cousin's shoulders for reassurance. They slide away from the pressure and Mitch's head lolls to one side. Blood is beginning to dribble from a minute wound between his eyes. A skilled job. The clamour of the engine idling is – to Reggie – only an extension of the uproar in his head. To have found Mitch and lost him irretrievably in less than an hour seems to the old man more than should be thrust on anyone. All possibility of an autumnal love is shattered by a chance bullet. Those two sentences convey some idea of Reggie's reactions, though not the fractured phrases in which he verbalises them. Soon he is considering whether the bullet had been as random as he had at first supposed.

He becomes aware of studded boots clattering across the tarmac. In the outer suburbs boots and bullets combined spell only one thing – a patrol of Street Wardens. Astounded by a strength he had thought spent long since, Reggie heaves himself into the empty coffin letting the lid lie just where it had tumbled. He closes his eyes to concentrate on controlling his breathing.

There are at first two voices arguing by the rear doors about the disposal of a couple of bodies. Reggie guesses the van – not Mitch – was the prize. Soon he hears a third voice. A girl – weeping – as she protests that Reggie is her grandfather. Though she seems plausible to the Wardens she has a harder moment or so convincing them she knows nothing of the driver.

Reggie admires the coolness with which she pleads her case. Between concentrating on his own breathing and evaluating how welcome a second bullet might be, he catches something of her explanation.

'Me and me brothers is orphans from the Urban War . . . that old feller brought us up . . . See? . . . You're joking! People poor as us can't afford luxuries like politics! So? What abart the van? Cheapest thing on offer in the weekly wall sheet, wasn't it? . . . 'Oo cares 'oo drives the bleeding thing? Not important with a 'earse is it? All I'm saying is we was told to rendezvous here. That's Grandad, an' that's all I know!'

Perhaps as eager to be rid of the bodies as to commandeer any roadworthy vehicle, the Street Wardens concede that Reggie may be removed provided the mourners are out of the sector by sundown. The argument reverts to Mitch's body. The girl – wisely it seems to Reggie – pretends disinterest. One Warden suggests it should be dumped at the crossroads pending identification from Regional Hall. Agreement at last. Or so the grunts imply.

Reggie senses the weeping girl standing over him. He is conscious of her hyacinth scent with each – he hopes – imperceptible intake of breath. Tears cool his tensed features as she whispers, 'Don't even breathe now. Ten seconds. We're carrying you out.'

With the coffin hoisted Reggie can relax sufficiently to register that his pall-bearers are moving off in slow march time. He hears the girl scream, and then a guffaw. His lips tighten as he guesses a Warden may have goosed her as she passed. Voices bickering over who should respray the van cross-fade and are lost in the steady crunch of footsteps below him. When he realises it is probably safe to open his eyes, they focus on the scabby trunks and tender leaves of plane trees.

At precisely which moment he could not swear a soft humming begins around him. The singing of anything other than sanitised doggerel is an imprisonable offence. Even to hum the melody that is becoming more identifiable each second is to incur the lost of a week's soya.

As gaps between detached rooftops become greater the humming grows more confident. First one and then two, then three, and finally six of the Freedom Brigade – all young enough to be his grandchildren, Reggie supposes – start to sing. Swallowing first to moisten his throat he adds his cracked baritone to their firmer voices. A brisk and chirpy chorus of *Oranges and Lemons* tints the sharp evening air.

THE CONTRIBUTORS

Keith Adamson has lived most of his thirty-seven years in Glasgow. He shares a mews cottage with his lover and their cat and he works in a small architectural practice. His extra-mural passions include computer programming and Shostakovitch.

Paul Davies was born in London but grew up in Bristol. He was educated at the Universities of Exeter and Sussex and wrote his Master's thesis on contemporary gay writing. He has worked as a journalist on *Capital Gay* and is a regular book reviewer for *Gay Times*. Now aged twenty-four, he is currently working on a first novel.

Martin Foreman was born in Scotland in 1952. His work experience includes a variety of jobs from cab-driving to being a waiter. His ultimate ambition is to be (simultaneously) rich, in love, and infinitely wise.

Paul Gurney has been unemployed and living in South London for four years. He writes when he feels like doing so. He is twenty-six years old.

Ian Hutson is twenty-six. He was born in Cleethorpes and has now returned there after an RAF 'gipsy' upbringing in Hong Kong. By day he is a civil servant but – at all other times – himself. His involuntary hobby is collecting memberships of minority groups.

Wyl Lawrence was born and raised in Pembrokeshire, South Wales. He graduated in Modern English at UWIST in Cardiff. For the past four years he has lived in the East Midlands where he is currently employed in the drugs field. His work has been published in *The National Gay*, *Gay News* and *I.P.B.M.*

James Macveigh is thirty-nine. He was born on Merseyside and is an ex-Borstal boy. He has worked as fairground assistant, building and factory labourer, dishwasher, barman, binman and waxworks attendant. He is now a businessman and the author of several stories as well as a biography, *Gaskin*, which was made into a BBC film.

Chris McVey is forty-three. He was born in Wallasey on Merseyside but now lives in Bristol with his wife and fourteen-your-old daughter. He began writing three years ago. He has had other stories published and is currently attempting a television play.

Joe Mills has had short stories published in *Gay News* and *Vulcan*. He was the winner of the 1985 *Gay Scotland* Short Story Competition. He is twenty-nine years old, both born and bred (to his great delight) in Glasgow where is now studying English Literature at the University.

Rodney Mills was a teacher for twenty-five years. He now cultivates his garden and other things. He lives just north of London and is working on a collection of stories and a novel.

Adrian Park was born in Preston, Lancashire, in 1953. Clydeside has been his adopted home for the past seven years and he currently teaches geology at the University of Glasgow. *Drafts* is his first published piece of fiction.

Chris Payne was born in Leeds in 1954, but now lives in London. He is concerned that so many gay people still have problems in coming out to themselves and to others. He greatly admires Chris Smith, M.P. He has had a story,

The Sighting, published in *Messer Rondo* (GMP, 1983).

David Rees's two most recent gay novels are *The Hunger* (GMP) and *Watershed* (Knights Press). He has also written many children's books. In 1978 he won the Carnegie Medal for *The Exeter Blitz*, and in 1980 the Other Award for *The Green Bough of Liberty*. He has recently moved to London, having lived for many years in Devon.

Philip Ridley was born in the East End of London where he still lives. His visual art has been widely and successfully exhibited in London since he graduated from St Martin's School of Art in 1983. He spent his early teens painting and writing lyrics for local punk bands. His first novel *Crocodilia* has just been published by Brilliance Books.

Peter Robins has published three collections of short stories, the most recent being *Our Hero Has Bad Breath* (Brilliance Books). His novel *Easy Stages* was published by GMP in 1985. He has had plays and stories broadcast and his work has been included in anthologies around the world. He has lived in South London for fifteen years.

Dave Royle is twenty-six. He was born in London and grew up in Suffolk. He graduated at Cambridge Technical College in 1982 and has since worked as an English teacher, a freelance researcher and journalist, and for a London Law Centre. He lives in South London.

Forthcoming Books
from Third House (Publishers)

TWOS AND THREES   David Rees
Vic, the central character in David Rees's new novel, is a middle-aged hunk who simply wants to grow old with his lover. Unfortunately he doesn't have one – at least not as he would define the word; only a succession of young men who want to share him with somebody else. Vic, in his adventures, is aided by his friend, camp Maurice, who writes Mills and Boon romances and whose success depends on his ability to turn the lives of his gay friends into straight fiction. The story has a bizarre twist when Vic finds he is the hero of Maurice's new novel . . . In turn serious and comic, this book is a delightful portrayal of the middle years of an attractive and vulnerable gay man.

'A first-class writer of enormous significance' —*Time Out*

To be published April 1987

SUMMER SHORTS Peter Robins
In 1977 Peter Robins' collection of stories *Undo Your Raincoats and Laugh* was published. It was the first book of short gay fiction to come out in Britain. *Summer Shorts*, his fourth collection, includes not only the polished satire that can be expected of him but perceptive observations of life in the chillier climate of the nineteen eighties.

'A master storyteller and humorist' —*Gay Times*

'Provocative and entertaining'—*New York Native*

' . . . has the ability to show, in a very few pages, how much the intrusion of a new and disturbing element (often sexual) can reveal about people'—*Body Politic*

To be published July 1987